Shadows in the Moonlight

Lila Montgomery

Contents

Chapter 1

Mirelle Austin.

Fake scenarios. When you think of it, it's almost like a dream, almost. I wish they were sometimes. So that I wouldn't have to close my eyes so tightly and pretend it happened. So that I'd actually feel it and live it. I dream of fantasy, fights, and princesses running away with swords. Princes who would sacrifice themselves for love. Will a prince even fight for me?

I could hear my parents yelling from the kitchen.

"How could you?"

"Relax, there's another chocolate bar on the counter."

God, it was eight in the morning.

They say you will only really rest in your grave, and honestly, that couldn't be more accurate.

I love my parents, I really do, they're just way too loud.

Even the Sun decided to rise in my face. the hair on my face turns to more ginger than brown in the sunlight, and I knew my hazel eyes would turn to honey-yellow. I flip my hair back, away from my face, and try to sleep again. But my phone rings.

What the hell does the world want from me?

"Hello?" I answered, not even knowing who's on the phone.

"Oh hey Mirelle, you know we're done with school and all. So, I'm throwing a party at nine pm. Want to join?"

Jenny.

Jenny and I have been best friends for a really long time, add to that she believes ninja turtles might actually exist, which is enough reason for me to be her friend.

I don't really have any friends at the moment, well except for Jenny. And I don't really mind it. Most of my school thinks I'm weird, so they keep their distance, and I keep mine. So for now, I only have that idiot of a human as my best friend.

"Jenny Hansen," I say. "You have all the seven days of the week, and all the hours of the day, and yet you chose Monday at eight am to invite me to your party."

She paused for a while, "...That doesn't answer my question."

I sighed. "Who's coming?"

"No one to worry about."

As much as I hate to admit it, I trust her. And to be honest, I have to get outside more often, so I don't see why not.

"I'm coming for the food. Get pizza."

I could hear her squealing from the other side of the phone. "Oh," she waited, "a little request, Mir?"

"What do you want?"

"Please don't dress like homeless people"

I smiled at that, "you know I'd do it just to embarrass the hell out of you"

She paused, "Okay then." She said calmly.

And she hung up.

That idiot just hung up on my face.

Oh, you're paying for that.

It took me a moment to realize I have to make an effort to go to this party. And I hate people, what the hell made me agree to that party?

Am I that indecisive? Actually no, I'm alright.

I scream internally and drag myself out of bed. I have just the right thing to wear, and I'll have to show off.

This is going to be one hell of a party.

My parents didn't look surprised at my outfit. Probably because they got used to my madness so that was the least they expected. Or they just thought I was stupid and didn't want to tell me.

Either way, I think I'm absolutely gorgeous.

I entered the party in my banana costume.

Everybody's eyes were on me. I mean, of course, it's pure beauty.

And then Jenny's eyes caught mine, and in a moment she was in front of me.

"What the hell!" she hissed, her thick brown curly hair jumping at her head movement.

"What?"

She stared at me with her brown eyes for a long while, and then she burst into laughter. She mustered herself enough to say, "have fun, queen!"

That's what I thought.

"Next time, hang up in my face again and I'll make potato chips from your bones."

She seemed to consider as she walked to the drinks. Waving her hand at me. Everyone was dancing or flirting with each other or fighting and I even saw somebody stuck in a chair.

But I went to the food. Priorities.

I ate. A lot.

That is why Jenny came to sit beside me. "Do your parents ever feed you?"

"They forget I exist sometimes."

She snorted, "Anyways, the party's over in 10 minutes-"

She stopped short as her eyes widened, I look in the direction she was looking at, and my breath stops.

"Well hey there, witch," Jack snarls. To me.

Jack...isn't really my favorite person. And I'm not his either, he and his circle don't have 'leaving me alone' on their to-do list. I'm not scared of him, Yet I always find myself vulnerable when he's around.

"Leave me alone, Jack." I tried my best to sound strong.

He gave me a mocking smile. "What are you wearing you weirdo?"

"Mind your business, how about that?" Jenny snapped at him.

His eyes switched to her. "Did I talk to you?" he said and took a step toward her.

I stretched my arm between them, "Jack please," I whispered.

"Didn't hear it."

I swallowed. "Please."

He looked me up and down. "No."

"Jack-" I said and put a hand on his shirt to push him.

But he just jumped to the back, "Ew, yo, she touched me!" he yelled to his friends. They all began making noises and looking at me like a fool.

Not wanting to deal with this any longer, I ran to the backyard. I sat down and closed my eyes.

It's okay.

They don't mean anything. I've been through worse. Even remember that time he said I was ugly? And I was strong enough to let it go so I can deal with it too. I'm a glowing star-

I felt light on my eyelids even though I was closing them, I tried to ignore it but I couldn't. I opened my eyes and blinked for few times.

I looked around, but there was nothing.

Then, there, at the farthest tree that leads to the wood, something- no it was someone with a cloaked figure. He held a blade. That reflected the light in my eyes.

A cloaked someone with a blade.

I tried to focus more on its facial features or anything but nothing, it was just a black figure. And as if it knew I was staring, it turned its head to the left and then right, and with a speed, I didn't even know was humanly possible, the person ran through the woods.

Now I have two options.

Either to run tell Jenny there was a thief in her house and leave it to the police.

Or pull out the Sherlock Holmes in me and go after him to be remembered as a legend and that's what a stupid person would do.

And of course, I chose option two.

What am I but stupid?

Chapter 2

I followed the figure through the woods. It was running, fast, and panting. And I was after it. Most of the tree branches crashed with my face. I looked up, I didn't know what time it was, but the moon was full, and the tall trees covered it. I didn't know where I was, but I knew it wasn't much away from Jenny's.

I kept running after it. Trying my best not to make any sound with my foot. My legs ached as if I didn't move for two years.

Well, it was true.

And it suddenly stopped at once, and I didn't move. Just hid behind a tree.

There was an empty spot, and in the middle, there was a huge wooden house. I'd say there were four who could live there.

What if it had ghosts, and the person was a witch.

No.

I continued to stare at the house, it was actually so beautiful. It was painted in a beautiful grey-black, its door and stairs were made of wood, it had a window right in the top middle that if it was mine I'd watch everything through it. If someone told me about this place I'd think that nobody lived here before, I mean it wasn't like any hunted houses. It didn't look too old or abandoned

Then there, slight light came from the window at the side of the house, there was life in it.

Then another figure appeared.

He was a middle-aged man. He had Grey-black hair and a beard. He didn't look too pleased though. But he wore a fake smile.

That was when the figure I followed removed his hood.

He had soft black obsidian hair that was as shiny as his blade, his eyes were deep blue I could drown in them if I stared long enough.

When he spoke, it felt like the trees themselves were quiet as if to hear his words being whispered.

He was...exquisite.

"Keir," the old man started devilishly.

Keir didn't answer him, only held a hateful look on his face.

"Keir," the man repeated, "I've grown tired of these games."

"Leave me alone," Keir spat.

"Oh gladly, but you remember our deal, don't you? And you know what they say, the deal is the deal."

Keir opened his mouth and closed it again. "I don't have it. I don't have the money for now."

The man took a step forward, "Pity, I guess now I have to take what's mine, your words aren't a man's words. Now, move aside so I can get inside the mess you call a house."

He's either stupid or blind.

"Wait," Keir gritted, "I can double them for you next month."

The man's smile grew wider. "Would you now? What makes me believe you? You don't even have the money this month, how will you have it the next one?"

"I'll work harder just...Please."

And as if the man never heard his pleadings he turned towards the wooden house.

Keir drove forward with his blade towards the man.

The man easily dodged him and laughed. "I know all your moves, Keir. It will take more than that to kill me." He took the blade from Keir's hand and pointed it to his throat. "I could kill you now with only one move." The man gritted on his teeth near Keir's ears so that he could hear his words clearly.

I had to stop him. I had to save that boy.

I'm a legend and if I die I'll be remembered as one. I wouldn't have liked my death to be any less mysterious anyway.

I took a long breath and moved away from the tree so they could see me, "Leave him alone!" I yelled with extreme confidence I didn't know I had.

The man looked at me and blinked. Then he laughed. Like hysterically laughed.

Keir's face paled.

"Excuse me it's just that...A banana?" he said through laughing

It took me a moment to realize that I am actually the banana-

Shit.

I try to have that neutral face they make in movies. "Let him go," I said intimidatingly, "or I'll call the cops."

I didn't even have my phone on me.

"Well I'm sorry to burst your bubble, lady but even if the cops came and took me, I'm not the only one who will come after him," he said with a smile.

"Then leave," I said harshly.

I wish I could have that confidence when I order a pizza. I'll try sounding dangerous next time.

If I lived.

The man let go of the boy. "I'll leave him." He took a step away from him and turned to Keir, "I'll come again in fifteen days. And if I didn't find the money which is, by the way, twice the amount, I'll take her and the other one."

The boy nodded and swallowed hard.

And the mean-looking man vanished through the darkness.

The boy blinked and slowly turned his gaze at me. I couldn't lift my eyes from the scar on his brow, then I searched all his face but no injuries could be found. He didn't look a lot older than me, I'd say he's nineteen or something. "Who are you?" He breathed.

I probably shouldn't tell him.

He had a knife though. "Mirelle." I smiled weakly.

He nodded briefly. "What are you doing here?"

I- does he really want to know I followed him all the way up to here to check if he wanted to kill Jenny?

"I was lost," I lied.

"In a banana costume?"

Someone throw me into a pit of mud.

"Thank you for what you did." He awkwardly looked at the ground.

"That's what legends do."

"What?"

"Nothing."

He cleared his throat. "It's late...do you need help to your home?"

"Uh, please?"

He smiled. "Of course, after all, I have to pay you back. Where's your house?"

What is the probability of him kidnapping me right in front of my house?

Watch me take my precautions. "Just follow me."

"Sure." He nodded and walked with me without speaking a word.

So I decided to speak. "So...who was that man?"

His face didn't change. "A wicked man."

Obviously.

"Yeah, now I know. Thank you."

He didn't care.

His hair is so cool.

Before I could say anything else, we'd already reached my home. "Thank you-"

"Listen, you should never tell anyone about this place or what happened and never come back ever again, do you understand?"

I nodded.

"Thank you," I tried again. Maybe he could be my friend.

"Swear it," he said with worry on his face. "Swear that you'll never tell anyone about there."

"I swear I won't tell a soul."

He nodded and in seconds he was gone like he was never there.

Chapter 3

We won't tell a soul.

"You mean to tell me that you followed someone into the woods with a banana costume just because he was standing in the backyard!" Jenny screamed.

"Pretty much," I said shoving a cookie into my mouth. And going back to reading my book.

Did I mention? I absolutely adore reading, it's like the only thing I can do.

Jenny stared at me with her dropped mouth, I just continued eating. "I- how do you feel?" she questioned.

"Powerful. I feel powerful."

She blinked. "What are you going to do?"

"Go there again of course."

"You- Answer me truthfully, are you insane?"

I stared at her for a long time. "Detective's work's never easy," I said dramatically and put the book by my side.

"Mirelle, not this nonsense again... you cannot be Sherlock Holmes!"

"Is it that obvious?"

"Yes." She stayed quiet for a while and I knew she was thinking. "I'm coming with you," she said steadily.

"No."

"No? What do you mean no? What if you died?"

"And this is, Jenny, exactly when you show up," I said. "First of all, you'll cry your eyes out and think about how much of a great friend I was."

"You weren't."

I glared at her but continued anyway. "Then you're going to tell my story to the whole world and tell them that heroes are never forgotten and that bravery is the key...and Sherlock Holmes."

"You can barely ask for extra ketchup."

"And yet I'm going after a guy with a dagger to save humanity," I sighed, "and my message for you Jenny, is to keep looking for ninja turtles."

She nodded and I pretended I saw tears in her eyes.

No time for feelings. I had to go.

I waited till dusk to move, maybe not the smartest idea but I didn't want anyone to see me.

I moved through the enormous trees with the smell of rain clutching my nose. It is beautiful, that's what I always thought, some stuff scares people simply because it's dark or lonely. But what if dark and lonely were all considered art? Will it still be considered scary?

I often think the night speaks more than day, and I always found comfort in it. Not fear.

Damn, I should write a book.

I kept walking. My feet stepped in water ponds, but still, I tried to make no sound on my feet, though I felt like every step made a sound a whole continent could hear.

I was nearly there when suddenly, I felt a light tug on my back.

That was it. I was going to die.

Where the hell was my parents, didn't they even think about where their poor child went off to?

God help me.

I wish Jenny doesn't mention that I got caught in the first two minutes.

"Move." A feminine voice ordered to my ear. "I have a dagger." I just obeyed quietly. She led us to...the house.

"Dylan!" She called.

In a moment, a boy came running out of the house, clutching a blade in his hands. He had chestnut skin and wide brown eyes that complimented his hair. He didn't look at all furious, his facial features were soft, curious, and a little bit excited. Just looking at him puts my mind at ease. Great, someone who's not angry.

But seriously though, What is wrong with them?

"I found her near the house," the girl said. Finally stepping in front of me.

Her pale pink skin glittered in the moonlight, and her eyes, her eyes were a chocolate brown. Her features were sharp with emotions but none of them were gentle. She was devastatingly beautiful.

She also looked like she wanted to kill me so yeah.

The boy eyed me. "What are we going to do with her?" he asked innocently.

"Tie her up to a chair till Keir arrives." She snapped her eyes back to me for a second. "She's probably one of Baron's dogs."

And before I tried to speak, they'd covered my mouth with a handkerchief.

Perfect.

We waited in silence, the only sound was the crackling fire they had on the green land. Thirty minutes passed, and here he was coming from a long distance with his hood on.

"Keir!" the boy yelled. And the other girl just rose to her feet.

As Keir approached us I really thought he would be kind and let me go, maybe even talk it out, but jokes on me he held a damn knife to my throat. The scar on his brow was even more noticeable as he came closer. "What are you doing here?" He hissed, "didn't I tell you to never come here again?"

"You met her before?" the boy asked, surprised.

Keir shot him a glare, and the girl removed the handkerchief from my mouth. "Speak," she commanded.

Oh, I was so done.

"Look," I began.

No, but like for real what the hell got me here?

"It isn't that I want anything with you it just-"

"Speak!" the girl repeated, but this time growing angrier.

God save me.

I'll die anyway, better say the truth and try not to go to hell. "I saw you," I said pointing to Keir. "You were at my friend's party with a cloak, I thought you were a criminal," I swallowed. "So I followed you to know exactly what you wanted and then that man showed and I thought I could stand up for you. With a banana costume." I managed an awkward laugh.

"Who showed up, Keir?" the boy interrogated. Keir didn't bother to even look at him.

I continued, "I wasn't lost, I just didn't want to tell you I followed you." I breathed. "And when you got me back home I kept thinking who you are and why you were there or if you were really someone with bad intentions towards my friend, so I came here the next day to see for myself, but she caught me," I said, pointing to the girl.

Keir just stared at me, scanning me up and down as if there were other viewable answers on me."Is that so?"

I nodded.

He seemed to consider as he took the knife away.

Thank God.

"Well, then I suppose you're no danger."

And it was quiet.

"I can't believe you walked all the way through the woods with a banana costume!" the boy beamed. So I joined him, I like this guy.

"I'm Dylan," he said after he stopped laughing. "C'mon Al, let her go."

"Idiot." She spat, still angry, "I told you not to trust people that easily."

"Oh, C'mon what kind of criminals would go on a mission as a banana? That's stupid."

I took that as a compliment.

"What's your name?" he said. Al looked him up and down. And turned to Keir with that look on her face as if to say 'kick him out.'

"Mirelle," I said anyways.

"It's nice to meet you, Mirelle!"

I smiled at his sweetness but I couldn't take my eyes away from the dagger he held.

"Oh, these? Don't worry...these are...nothing." He hid it behind his back.

"Yeah, not weird at all."

"If weird was a competition those people would win," he said with a hand over his mouth so the others wouldn't listen, though it was clear they did.

The air blew harder against my skin and it made me shiver, I couldn't tell if it was also because those three people were staring into my soul.

"Anyway." Dylan stopped talking. "Oh, are you hungry? You seem tired."

I was. But I also wanted to have a little distance away from them. "Yes! I mean if it's okay with you of course."

"Sure, sure. Come inside." His smile grew wider as he cut the ropes that tied me with his blade. We strode towards the house as Al and Keir's eyes never left us.

It's just as big as I thought, there were a lot of rooms, and the house was just a beauty. I wanted to take a tour around but Dylan only led me to the kitchen.

"We have pizza. Is that okay with you?"

"That will be perfect," I smiled. "Are you sure it's alright?"

"Yeah sure, we don't have any guests here often so we actually enjoy having people over." He waited. "So, look, I know you probably don't like Keir right now but-" He said as he heated the pizza.

"What? No! I actually tried to be his friend but he...well."

"Isn't the best communicator," he continued for me, "well I apologize for what we've put you through earlier, as I said before we're not used to having guests at all and most of the people who visit are...well- bad guys." His face darkened at that. "You met him, didn't you? In the woods."

"Yes, that man-"

"Baron, his name is Baron."

I stayed silent as I took a bite. "Who is he?"

He sighed. "I don't think it's my thing to share."

"I understand," I said though I truly didn't. We both stayed silent for a while. "So you and Keir are friends?"

"He's the only family I have, him and Alana," he said, rubbing his neck.

"You seem close." I agreed.

"We've been living together for nearly three years." He shook his head. "And maybe they're even the only friends I have. But you know."

He seemed too good for this world. And well who am I to leave him like that? "Wanna be friends, Dylan?"

He smiled excitedly, "yes!" he laughed. "You know I was actually going to ask you that the moment you mentioned the banana costume."

I covered my face with my hands. "This is going to chase me throughout my entire life."

"You should be proud."

He understands me. He's great.

"Let's get outside; they're probably wondering what's taking us too long." He gestured to me to follow him, giving me another slice of pizza in my hand.

Outside, I found Al staring at me as if she was waiting to freak the hell out of me. This woman is scary. Keir was still beside her.

I owed him an apology. All of them. "Listen, guys," I said, "I know this isn't the best way you could meet someone, and I'm truly sorry about it, and if you like it...I won't come here again, sorry to interrupt."

"No!" Dylan blurted, "You should visit again. Please Keir," he said looking at him.

Keir nodded and...smiled. "I supposed this is the least I could do. After all, you did help that day."

I smiled then. "Same for you, you know where to visit Keir." He nodded firmly.

"It was nice to meet you all," I said looking at the three of them. "And I apologize for the discomfort I caused again."

They all smiled. Except for Al.

"I should go; my family's probably looking for me."

As if.

"You sure you don't need anyone to walk you home? It's late," said Keir.

"I should be okay. It's not away from here."

"Take care then."

I nodded and strode to the woods as I felt their gazes on my back.

Chapter 4

Keir Striker.

I still don't trust her...

However, it's the only way to know if she's someone with Baron, I'll make her think we trust her, and then strike.

I've had enough.

He's acting like it's his right to manipulate us. As if we already didn't have enough from life.

I sat on the kitchen counter and poured myself a drink.

"What did he say?" Alana said quietly but not weakly, folding her arms and resting on the kitchen's door frame. Again, believing it's her fault. "And why didn't you tell us?"

"Nothing to concern you," I replied, "I- I didn't want it to be a burden on you."

Her nose flared. "You promised," she said with a finger pointed at me. "You promised you would consider me in everything, you promised you wouldn't leave me behind." She dropped her hand. "you promised."

Even now, I can't look her in the eyes and tell her I'm sorry, I wouldn't dare. "He," I gulped, "he wanted the money, and I didn't have it, he threatened to take you back and Dylan with you and I couldn't do anything. I just begged him but he didn't show a Flecker of emotion.

"He tried to get to you, I tried to reach my dagger and stop him but he took my dagger and he was..." I couldn't continue anymore as I rubbed my eyes.

Al just stared, with mouth open, slightly.

"It isn't your fault," she whispered.

"Neither is it yours," I whispered back, resting my head on the counter.

"What did you tell him?" She said, "he didn't just let you go out of kindness, did he?"

"That girl showed up, Mirelle. She told him to let me go and leave."

"And he did?" She asked, arching her brow.

"He did. But it's not that easy, he told me if I didn't have twice the money in fifteen days he's going to take what's his." I stared at her. "As if."

"I hate that bastard," Al gritted.

"We all do," I said, stepping away from the counter. "But what's hate going to do?"

I offered her a drink, which she gladly accepted and brought to her lips.

"So what's with the girl?" She asked more command than a question.

"I don't trust her."

"Me neither. She's a spy, isn't she?"

I shrugged, "I'm not sure, but let her come here and believe we trust her, and then when we're sure, we're going to get the information out of her."

Al nodded in agreement.

"Do you have the money?" she asked after a long pause.

"Only the half," I confessed.

"Listen," she began. "I thought this through really well, and I've decided it. If you didn't have the money next time I'll just go with him. Don't try to stop me," she said with a neutral face. "I'll still find a way to pay you back. Just Let me put an end to this nonsense if I can."

"You're bluffing-"

"I'm serious. I survived the past and I can do it again. It will be better for everyone anyway."

"Listen to me, Alana. You're speaking nonsense now. You can't just go throw yourself to hell because you think it's for the better. We're doing everything for all of us. Not just for you. It's not your fault and it will never be. So stop fooling around and fight."

She just stared at me, into my soul.

I wouldn't doubt she'd frighten Baron to his death.

She nodded and strode to her room.

fight.

Al wasn't the only one who needed those words. We will survive this, we all will. We survived worst than this.

Fool.

He thinks he can take her as if she's his, think he can torture her with his wretched dirty work.

A stupid fool.

I will destroy him.

I'll make him wish he never existed, and I'll gladly laugh as he does. But for now, let me just enjoy my drink and not worry about it.

Alana Li.

I don't know what to do anymore.

Should I just kill him and be done with it? Poison would do.

I can't help but blame myself for everything. After all, I got myself into that stupid fight.

You're a disappointment.

My mother was probably right, I am indeed a disappointment. Still, that doesn't give Baron the rights to that.

I can't stop them. These Thoughts are louder than I could fight them. I can't help but remind myself how reckless and stupid I was.

I was twelve. A child.

And they tried to reshape me as they please.

They said I was a stupid, ungrateful child just because I was different and I have been trying all those years to prove them wrong, to be worthy of their acceptance, but it was no good.

They thought I was a disappointment.

So I became one.

A failure, I failed all my classes on purpose.

Ungrateful, I didn't come home till midnight.

Emotionless, I was the meanest I could be.

A disappointment, I became their worst nightmare.

My father's from Japan and my mother's American. My father moved to America with his family, and that's when they supposedly "fell in love" they got my older brother, Haru and then they got me.

It was always him that they loved more. It's not like he cared, he moved at the first opportunity possible and now he's a doctor. Haru was the only one I got to complain to him about the shit my parents put me through, and to his credit, he agreed.

I was sixteen when it happened.

I was back from school, "Hey, Alana!" a familiar voice yelled over to me.

Smiling at myself I turned to face the only friend I had in school, "Amy."

She was biting on some kind of snacks. "Want some?" she offered.

I shook my head. "I'm good. I just really wish I could see you once and you wouldn't be eating those."

She raised her finger taking another bite. "Don't you dare say a word about my airheads." She squeezed her stomach. "They gave me all these, why shouldn't I eat more of them? You want to know what I named this big belly there?" she asked jokingly.

I laughed. "What?"

"King Jarry the third."

"You named your belly King Jarry the third?"

"Yup! He doesn't deserve to be treated any less."

I rolled my eyes at her silliness. "Anyways, see you tomorrow. I have to go."

She smiled, "bye!"

I Waved at her and walked to my house.

And then it all happened.

Two men showed up out of nowhere and tried to...touch me. I had a glass bottle so I smashed his head with it. There was so much blood I thought I was going to collapse. I had no time to run, no time to think. The other one shoved me in a car and injected me with something that I lost consciousness.

When I woke up I was in an empty room, hands and legs tied. It was horrific, it was absolutely horrific. I sat straight. Trying my best to let in any oxygen inside my lungs. But I struggled to breathe.

But then a man, tall and big. The wickedness of his face couldn't have been more obvious. He entered the room with two others.

"Good nap?" he said with an evil grin.

"Who are you?" I spat.

"Leave that." He said, his eyes fully scanning me. "Who are you?"

"Let me go!" I screamed, losing it.

"Listen here, Alana Li. I know who you are, I know who your parents are, and I know everything about you, so sit like humans do and listen to what I have to say."

Tears covered my face, I was a mess.

I didn't understand anything. One moment I was going home and the other I'm here with a strange man.

I sat straight, still sobbing. "Please, let me go," I mumbled.

"I'm afraid that can't happen," he answered neutrally.

Fear throbbed inside my body, and he smiled because he was aware of it.

"Now." He knelt to scan my face. "Tell me what happened back there."

He must have seen the confusion in my eyes. "You know, the man you nearly killed with your bottle."

I understood now, but still, I didn't answer.

"He was going to die, you know, all because of you."

I sucked in my breath.

A criminal.

That is what I was.

"Now, just to assure you, he did survive." His eyes slid to the ties on my foot, "but unfortunately, he was one of my men. So you have two options, Alana." His eyes now looking at mine. "Either you stay here and do whatever I tell you to pay your debt, or your friend...What's her name again? Oh, Amy, will have to be the one paying the price. "

I spat on his face.

"Bad girl," he said and simply wiped it off with his pocket square.

He gestured to one of the men who were standing, and the man handed him a tablet.

"You see that green paper?" he asked, pointing to the paper showing on the screen. "Douglas there will drive you to a building, you get inside, grab the paper and go back to the car understood?"

I couldn't even answer or move my head, I just lied on the floor and...wept. I could feel them all leaving the room. And the room darkened as I cried.

The next day someone entered the room to tell me where to find that damn paper. And we drove to the building, I did everything I could.

And here it was, the paper left on the table, I shoved it inside my pocket and returned as swiftly as I came, and back to the car.

"Did you get it?" Was the first thing Douglas asked.

I nodded.

"Good," he said with a smile.

"Are there any cameras?" I asked

"All taken care of."

And we drove back to the room. Thoughts were too heavy for my brain. All of them were just accusations that I was stupid. I mean look at what I've gotten myself into. But atleast...these thoughts were trapped, trapped too deep in my mind I don't think they're ever going to get out. Trapped...just like me.

"I see you did a great job." That big man said once we arrived.

I didn't answer. I wasn't really planning to.

"Good then," he said and left.

And it has been this way for months. Just me doing his dirty work. Stealing, spying, hurting, and getting hurt. And mostly hating myself.

I need someone to help me. Anyone.

Just help.

One day, I actually dared to request such a thing. "I've done everything you asked, please," I swallowed. "Please, Baron, let me have one day, just one day a week."

I hate it when I beg.

He scanned me. "I knew you would ask." His eyes never leaving mine. "Very well, but if you considered doing anything-"

"I won't. I promise. I know whose life's on the line."

"You have the Fridays then," he said at last.

I nodded and strode out of his office.

Good. Better than nothing. All I have to do is tell my parents and Haru that I'm okay. Not that I think my parents would care.

Chapter 5

Mirelle.

What on earth am I supposed to do with my life?

I'd like to stay home and read, but now...I honestly don't know why I do this to myself. I just finished reading my book and I...I'm crushed. I hate it when I feel like it's over, you've gotten invested with the characters, and you care about them and love what they love and hate what they hate. You feel like you fight alongside them and genuinely feel happy for them when they're happy.

I think I like them because I want to be one of them, or at least just like them, I want to experience what they experience, I want to stand on a hill with the wind ruffling my hair back in a main-character moment, and I want to be that deadly woman everyone is scared of. I don't want to give my heart to anyone; fearing they will break it, but I want to do it accidentally, dreadfully, I want to be mad at myself for falling in love, I want it then to turn into poetry and metaphors of sweet angry words. When I fall in love I want it to be thrilling. I want the readers of my life to seek more, to be like me.

But this is nonsense. This isn't life. I have to wake up from this ridiculous dream.

And I know they're not real, but I just can't help but miss them.

I need to get out of bed or I'll cry. I also want pizza. And ranch.

I called jenny moments ago but she didn't answer the phone.

Fake.

I forced myself out of bed and walked to the kitchen, "Mom!" I yelled even though she's inches away.

"What do you want?"

I wrapped my arm around her shoulder like the besties we are. "Do we have food?"

"No," she said without lifting her eyes from her phone. "Go get yourself some."

"Mother, I am your daughter. You should feed me."

She gave me a look of disgust that let me know I had to go within thirty seconds if I cared for my life.

So I did.

I walked all the way to the grocery store with nothing to think of but my book, my hunger for food and emotions, and a certain family in the middle of the woods.

I made one decision during my visit to this grocery store: Food is one of the most beautiful things about life.

Why does walking with a cart feels very shameful? Why does everyone have to scan me from head to toe like I'm their sister-in-law? And then we have to stare at each other's faces for two minutes straight cause our carts crashed in opposite ways and we don't know who should go first. I'm probably overthinking this. Anyway, I've got Cheetos, ramen, Doritos, and pizza. I'm going to die, there isn't one single healthy thing in all of these.

Pizza.

I took my phone and dialed my mom.

"Mom, I'm going to be late today so don't worry about me."

"I won't, let them take you if possible," she answered.

"Very funny."

"I know, right?"

"Have a good day, mom."

"Oh, I will without you complaining around," she said it seriously but I could feel her smile through the phone.

I love that woman.

"Dylan!" I call when I came nearest to the house, feeling a smile already making its way onto my face. Seconds later, Dylan came running out of the house, smiling.

"Hello!" I squealed.

Dylan helped me with the bags and said, "We were bored in there, good thing you came." He banged my shoulder with his.

"I got pizza!"

"You shouldn't have," he said, with that kind smile of his.

"And not just that but also...Doritos."

His jaw dropped. "You have? Thank you, I love Doritos! Keir!"

Keir instantly came out of the house this time wearing a normal dark grey sweatshirt and pants. Al follows, she didn't even try to smile, maybe I shouldn't expect her to. Keir scanned me up and down then smiled, slightly.

"Hello, you two!" I greeted.

"Hello, Mirelle," Keir greeted back calmly. "What brings you here? If you don't mind me asking."

Does he want to kick me out? Or is it just me?

"Nothing really, I just figured I can come over with some snacks and...well when we first met it wasn't a very unique way so... I figured I could make that up."

Why does Alana look at me like I'm a human with a horse's head?

He arched his brows. "You're very welcome then."

"Thanks," I said, trying to act like shy girls and hide the fact that I'm hungry as hell.

We just stood there staring at each other.

That's when Dylan said, "oh C'mon we're not going to stand here forever." He took the food out of the bag and placed it on the grass and then went to grab two wooden sticks to set fire. It actually worked.

Impressive.

He got a speaker and played some music. "Sit down, Y'all." It seemed Alana wasn't really the kind of person to be commanded because she drew out her dagger but put it back down when Keir gave her a single glance.

We were done eating when Dylan suddenly just stood up and started dancing. He took Alana's hand and danced and jumped, completely ignoring her hissing at him.

"C'mon Keir, this is fun!" Dylan called.

"I'm okay," he said and stayed right where he is, but the light and amusement in his eyes were impossible not to notice.

I think somewhere in this Alana actually, smiled.

I just watched them. It wasn't so often that I came across people like them, full of love and caring for each other, even if they didn't like to show it.

One day, maybe one day, I'd dance around with the people I love like they're all I had, even if it didn't happen, watching them is...pleasing, just like in books.

Night fell and it was then, that Dylan came to sit beside me to watch the fire.

"It's beautiful, isn't it?

"Yeah," I said, resting my head in my hands. I know I shouldn't approach the matter so fast, and I know it's none of my business but I've been watching him as Alana, and Dylan danced, it seemed as if something upset him, so maybe I should just ask Dylan if maybe I should treat him more...I don't know. Differently?

"Is he always like this? He doesn't seem so happy," I said, looking at Keir who already was staring at me from a longer distance.

Dylan sighed, "it's not that he's not happy he's- listen, Mirelle. I know he might seem rude but isn't! Look he- he saved me. I grew up in the streets. I didn't know anything except for my mother and my name, and even one day...she disappeared out of nowhere." He looked down at the floor and his voice lowered.

"I tried to work but I was either manipulated or rejected. I tried everything but...nothing worked. Then, one day, Keir saw me in a store, how helpless I was. He waited for me outside and...we talked. We kept talking for a long time and then, he offered me to come to live here. I couldn't even believe it, I thought it was one of those dreams I had when I slept on the sidewalks, even now, I still can't believe God listened to all my prayers that I thought no one could hear but myself.

"So I'm sorry if you think he's...rude. He's just isn't really comfortable around new people, but if you get to know him, you'll find that he's the kindest and nicest person you could ever meet."

I nod and continue6 to watch the fire. Just the fire, of course. I rest my hand on Dylan's back, finding that this is the best way is comfort him.

If Keir's really like that... Then I don't see why not try harder and be his friend. A leaner touch could let him relent. It's when I feel a presence beside me that I'm awoken from my thoughts.

Keir stood there, "Why don't you tell us about yourself a little, Mirelle," he looked startled when I looked at him, but he smiled as if proud of himself he came up with such a question and took place beside me.

"Yeah! I've told you, now it's your turn." Dylan clapped his hands.

"Sure. I mean there is nothing to tell but," I pause, "I don't know how to do anything special I mean...I'm not talented with anything, I don't have any special hobbies, I just do everything thing for fun.

I only have one good friend the others either left silently or chaotically and I have good parents and I- live, I love to live and I love life, I love nature. But I like reading. I like reading and poetry." I finished and looked at the ground, letting the awkwardness eat my head. I lifted my head and Keir's eyes locked with mine. It's like he's trying to figure out something, and only the inside of my eyes had that answer. He was confused like he could come closer for a better look but...there's that something. All I tried to do was just soften my eyes, to try and look 'friendly' enough. Though he didn't take his eyes off mine.

It's his language then, huh?

"Thanks for sharing," Keir said at last.

"Of course." I smiled, though I sense something is off with him.

Keir.

For a moment I was jealous of her.

A free soul living instead of waiting to live.

So for a brief moment, even if it was just a few minutes, I allow myself to believe her, to think that what she just said is real.

How?

How did she do that?

Did she mourn those friends who left she speaks of? Did she even allow herself to feel it? The heartbreak.

Teach me. Teach me how to do what you did if what you said is true, spy.

At that moment she looked at me, it seemed as if she heard what I was thinking, but she turns her head.

As if.

As if I'm able of letting anyone in. Specifically a spy.

But what if she wasn't?

What if she was just the girl she assumed she was? What if she was just a girl who helped me this day, a girl who Dylan loved in a few minutes, a girl who lived just because she wished to experience?

I don't let myself think any much more than this. I would regret this if she hurts them, wouldn't I? So I just consider watching her carefully. That's a wise choice.

It's midnight when she rose to leave, so I offered to take her. To my surprise, she accepted.

We walk through the woods, my dagger clutched to my side, of course. Why does my stupid heart-

"So," she said, startling my thoughts, "are you planning to tell me what's the daggers deal?"

Nosy.

But telling her wouldn't be a problem, would it? After all, Baron knows all of that. "Every one of us came here in a...tragic way, so we just... we learned how to fight with it." My voice came out coarse.

"Hmm," she waited, "how?"

"My mother, she thought I could learn fighting, it was me who suggested it actually, but she welcomed the idea and found me a tutor to help me."

"You love her, huh?"

"I do, she was one of the people who saw the light out of all the darkness." I tried to sound formal but I couldn't help the awe that was in my voice.

"And...you taught Dylan and Alana?"

"I did."

"That's very noble of you, no wonder they love you so much," she said as she lead me to her house. She extended a hand to touch my arm but I walked faster and tried not to be close enough.

I didn't answer her though, we finally arrive at her house. Simple indeed. But still, could be a stopping point.

"Thank you, Keir."

"Of course."

"It was nice to meet you all again." She tilted her head to the side.

"You were nice company too." I kept telling myself that she was just acting. But she kept acting way too well.

Maybe she's just-

Get ahold of yourself, Keir.

She smiled and searched for her house keys in her bag.

That's it? I have to know more. I have to catch her, to stop her, I have to startle her, to let her know I know exactly what she thinks I don't.

Who are you, spy?

"Wait," I said and she lifted her head. "There's this party we have each month, normally it's just the three of us but. It would be nice if you joined. It's next Friday at eleven pm."

Her eyes sparkled. "Yes. I would love to." she smiled. "And tell Dylan it was nice seeing him...and Al too."

I nodded as she entered her house and locks her house.

I will catch her.

And I'll make her regret the day she decided to enter this house.

Chapter 6

Mirelle.

"So," Jenny said as she took a bite from her McChicken, "are you really going?"

"Of course I am."

She stopped eating, "Why?"

"I like them."

"Mirelle, what if they hurt you?"

"What-"

"I mean people don't just go into the woods with only three people with daggers just because they like them."

I stared at her for a while. Then shook my head, knowing that's just out of love. "Look, Jenny, I know you're worried but they're pretty nice and they won't hurt me, I mean you've got to meet Dylan he's like the nicest ever."

She took an aggressive sip from her milkshake. "You know what? I warned you. Do whatever you like, but if you die I'll tell everyone that you were a trashy stubborn idiot."

"Fine!"

"Fine!"

We didn't make eye contact and just folded our arms.

So she wants to be mad right now? Oh Fine! I'll be more than happy-

"The fries are really good though."

"I know right," I said shoving one in my mouth.

Friday, 11 pm.

The old tree above me shielded the light from fully reaching me.

I was walking cautiously, trying not to step into any little pond so it wouldn't mess up my red jumpsuit And also the book I held tightly to my chest. I know he said a party but dresses are not my cup of tea.

I was busy watching the trees when I heard steps, not human, approaching.

It came closer. I stayed still.

Is it a vampire? God, I'm grateful for anything but not getting killed by a vampire.

It ran faster and got closer, at some point I heard its steps stop but then it continued, and that's when I saw it.

It was a doe.

And I screamed.

I didn't scream because I was scared of it, I screamed because a knife soared and hit the doe's legs, it fell.

Then three cloaked figures appeared. The first one had ropes twisted around the two trees the doe was between, the second figure took another batch of ropes and twisted it around the deer's legs; The third figure stepped inside the rope like-ring and stabbed the doe till the light left its eyes.

It was dead.

The cloaked people now took off their hoods. And it was-

I screamed again.

"Calm down, it's okay," Dylan said, raising his arms in assurance.

I couldn't I was panting so badly. There was blood and a dead deer.

"Ugh just shut up, no one told you to come early," Alana snapped and glared at Keir to say something.

Keir just looked at me, thinking, calculating. his mind in a different place. Alana stopped talking, the only sign of her understanding.

"Were you surprised?" Keir asked gently.

I nodded.

"Well, I'm sorry we startled you." He pointed to the house with his head. "We can get inside." And they all headed towards the house, one by one so I followed. Though Dylan waited behind, near the doe. When we arrived I sat in a big armchair. Al and Keir sat on the opposite sofa.

"You didn't think we just sat here and had the money, did you?" he sighed, "We don't only have daggers to fight with it, we hunt and then sell them to the merchants. As Al said, you were not supposed to see that, we tend to hide the whole process from people's eyes to avoid reactions like yours," he said so calmly.

"I'm okay," I managed.

"Your face looks whiter than none baked bread," Dylan squinted his eyes at my face as he rested his back on the door.

I managed a smile.

"Do you need some water?" he asked.

"Yes, please."

"Just a second," he said and headed to the kitchen.

Keir came and sat beside me. "May I ask what you're reading?"

I handed him my book. Emily Dickinson poems.

He read the title and surprise filled his features, he looked as though this was the last thing he thought a girl like me would read. As if. I may seem as if I'm dumb but at least I have a good taste in literature. He opened the book, it stopped at one of my favorite poems.

Hope is the thing with feathers That perches in the soul, And sings the tune without the words, And never stops at all,

And sweetest in the gale is heard; And sore must be the stormThat could abash the little birdThat kept so many warm.

I've heard it in the chillest land, And on the strangest sea;Yet, never, in extremity,It asked a crumb of me.

He read it, and the glitter in his eyes couldn't be missed, though it disappeared shortly after. "You like poetry?"

"I do. Do you?"

He nodded and smiled to himself. "What do you like reading about?"

I paused to think. "You see, if we're talking about poetry, then I like to read sad poems and ones about life and love."

"I see." He read a few pages silently.

So I cleared my throat, "I'm sorry...about my reaction," I finally said.

"No worries," Keir said with a faint smile. He handed me the book. "What's important is not to go tell someone else."

"Sure, sure I mean why would someone even want to know that." I awkwardly laughed.

He shrugged and opened his mouth to say something else, but Dylan came with a glass of water.

He handed it to me and said, "so forget what just happened, today is going to be a bummer." He leaned in to whisper in my ear, "I literally can't believe Keir invited you."

"Everyone can hear you," Al said, and Keir nodded in confirmation.

"Well it's no secret, everybody knows Keir would kick me out."

"Then maybe you deserve it."

"I just spilled two drops of milk on the counter!" Dylan snapped.

Al opened her mouth to speak but Keir interrupted, "please stop fighting, I can't stand your irritating voices. Besides, we have guests," he said, looking at me. I smiled at them.

"Keir is right, shut up Dylan," Al mumbled.

It was three pm by the time they were done doing the preparations for their party. "It's a surprise," Dylan had said and so I stayed in the house, Keir and Al coming in every while to check on me.

And then finally, Dylan came in to take me outside. When I came out of the house, the first thing I saw was a cake but there were decorations though, good ones. There was a huge bull's-eye. And there were eight trees, every two trees were tied together with a red satin ribbon. There were a lot of cushions and blankets placed around the fire they lit on the ground.

"What do you think?" Dylan asked merrily.

"It's beautiful," I responded, still admiring the place.

"I'm hungry-"

"You're always hungry," Al hissed from over the table.

Dylan ignored her, "C'mon Mirelle, let's go eat, you must be starving." he stretched his arm for me so I took it.

When everyone was done eating, they all stood up and stared at each other with mean smiles.

"What are you- wait is this some kind of witch ritual thing?"

Al snorted but didn't lift her eyes from the other two.

"Mirelle, see that red ribbon?" Dylan said, with a serious tone.

"Yes."

"Go stand there, cause things are about to get wild." I didn't understand a thing but I did as he said anyway.

They stood like that for another five seconds and then. "Go!" Keir shouted, and scared the hell out of me and they all ran towards the trees with the ribbons so suddenly and scared the hell out of me again. They crossed the red ribbon on each of their trees and Dylan shouted to me, "Run!"

"What?" I yelled back.

"Run!"

"To where?"

"To another ribbon. When you reach it come back to this one. It's a race!"

They were all so fast I didn't think I could reach any of them, but I ran.

And I wish I didn't.

My legs ached after running for about two minutes, I was out of breath, but I saw the ribbon, and I turned around to get back.

God help me I'm just a poor sick girl.

I did return though, but everyone was there already and I couldn't take it anymore. I collapsed on the floor. "Why?" I squealed.

No one cared about the fact that I was on the ground, probably dying.Though Dylan only laughed.

"Do you actually have the nerve to laugh when you lost?" Al asked grinning.

"At least I wasn't the last one."

"Wait, who won?" I still couldn't get up.

"Keir, of course then Al then me, and lastly, you," he said, and there was a look of pride on Keir's face.

Cool people lose in races.

"I- someone helps me."

Al snorted. "Are you that out of shape?"

"Excuse me if I don't fight and hunt with a dagger and scare people." She just laughed and extended a hand. And I took it.

Good. She began to like me.

"It isn't over yet," Dylan announced.

"What?" I breathed.

"Everybody, prepare your daggers," Keir commanded. And I knew I had to shield my head if I wanted to live. I could hear the sound of something soaring and then it slammed into something hard.

"It's over," Dylan said. And I slowly removed my hands from over my head.

It was their daggers that slammed the bull's-eyes on the tree. It was Keir's dagger that hit the right point. Dylan's closest to it and Al was the furthest, though I was still impressed.

"Loser," Dylan teased.

"Shut up."

Dylan's eyes beamed as he snapped them to me. "Do you want to try, Mirelle?"

"Maybe-"

"Here, take mine." Keir extended his dagger, and I took it. It was heavier than I expected, so I held it tight.

"No, don't press it too hard, and don't let it too loose either." He instructed, "Straighten your back and come closer to the target." I took two steps to the front.

"Now put the end of the handle right into your palm, close it with your middle finger. Great, now put your index finger on the spine, where you balance the dagger." I thought it was going to cut me but it actually didn't.

"Put your arms to the back. Inches behind your head."

I tried, "like that?"

He glanced a look at Dylan, and Dylan nodded and came.

"May I?" Dylan asked before putting his hands on my elbow. I nodded, and he lifted my elbow a little more to the back and stepped away.

"Good," Keir said. "Now throw, release it with your index finger."

I expected it to fall, or maybe fly in the opposite direction and hit my face, but instead, I heard Dylan cheering, so I looked and it was just a few inches away from Al's, right at the corner.

I actually freaking did it.

"Great job, Mirelle!" Dylan beamed.

I blinked a few times at the dagger. "I feel like Batman."

"And how does Al feel about what just happened?" Dylan asked Alana with a teasing smile.

"Like I wanna punch your face till you shut up," she answered neutrally.

"Thank you."

She shoved him off with a hand and went to sit near the fire, Dylan still followed her as if nothing had happened like a lost puppy. Keir grabbed his knife and returned to join them but said, "that was a good one for a beginner." He smiled. And I smiled back, trying my best to hide the blush on my cheeks, and went after him.

"Wait here." Dylan rose to get something from the house.

He returned with a violin.

"Wait, you play the violin!" I asked.

"You know, I'm quite the artist here." Dylan smiled.

"Play something."

He took his bow and swung it on the violin's strings. Like a dance, a beautiful, organized dance. With every move of his arm, a delightful melody was born. I stretched my back on the cushions, and let my soul be a part of the music, my heart sings along, and my fingers danced with the melody. I stared at the stars and imagined stories in their place, shy and romantic. Outgoing and tragic. Fighters and broken ones.

I glanced at Keir to find him already looking at the stars. Is he thinking what I'm thinking? Maybe he's just shy. And needs a nudge to the light. Maybe I could help him-

He turned to me and his eyes widened as he caught me staring. I quickly turned my head back to the sky.

The last thing I remember I saw was the stars dancing to the music.

Chapter 7

Mirelle.

I woke up at Keir's house.

Dylan and Alana were sleeping on the scattered cushions.

But Keir-

I turned around to see Keir sitting on a chair, Staring. "Good morning," he said with a soft smile.

"Good morning." I smiled awkwardly. Then it hit me "Oh my God! I'm so sorry, I didn't mean to fall asleep-" I rose rapidly to my feet.

"No, it's alright," he said, standing too. "You can stay for a while before you go, it's still early."

"No. No, I should be leaving, my parents are probably worried about where I am, what time is it anyway?"

"It's just eight, and truly, it's okay, no need to panic." He chuckled.

It's the first time I hear him chuckle, I didn't realize I thought they weren't capable of being happy. So I laughed in return, having nothing else to consciously give back.

"Come with me, you have to eat something before you go," he said. I nodded and followed him to the kitchen.

"I can manage on my own, you don't need to-"

"Please." He smiled, "I would like you to know that I have many other talents other than throwing a knife and murdering innocent animals."

"Why did nobody tell me about your sense of humor?" I said with a laugh.

His smiling eyes scanned my face from up and down, and then, as if remembering something unpleasant, he swallowed and turned to what he was doing. But he eventually smiled and said, "Your parents, you don't talk about them so much,", he asked as he cooked the omelet.

Well, that came out out of nowhere, but well he started a conversation on his own. "What? No, they're nice people, you can say they love each other to no end, but being with them is like watching the live-action to tom and Jerry." I chuckled, "They love me, they really do but sometimes I just feel they found me in a kinder surprise egg."

He laughed, and set the omelet on a plate, placed a glass of Orange juice, and cut some apples. "And, voila!"

I admired the plate first, and then dug in and was fully satisfied.

"That was epic," I smiled at him, rubbing my belly. I tried to touch his arm as a thank you, but he flinched away. I didn't understand what I did wrong so I just said, "I'm sorry-"

"it's alright," he said instantly. "And you're welcome, it's the least I could do." I nodded quietly. And we just stayed silent.

"What about yours? if you don't mind me asking, you told me about your mom before."

His eyes twitched, "My father's not here, he left us a few years ago, it was my mother and me in her house. That's when I decided I should move here.

"It was quieter and calm. And mom supported it. So I did." He had a sad smile on his face.

I took a sip of my orange juice, a bit too invested now. "Is that house yours?"

He shook his head. "No, it's my father's we used to come here a lot when we needed some quiet. But...he left and he hadn't visited here ever since."

"I like it. I like the place," I said cheerfully hoping to pass my energy to him

He giggled, "I'm glad you do."

A loud bird's shrieking could be heard from outside, and the cold breeze passed down my spine, sending shivers I could hear more than feel in such quietness that now was set between the both of us.

I sit casually as if I'm not fighting everything in me to look at him. He can have his privacy for a moment without my eyes in his business always asking for a reaction out of him-

Well, I looked at him now, what is there to be done.

And boy did he like right back. How does he even do it? Does he have an eye in the back of his head always looking at me? Well, that's a bit too much but it's fine.

Am I happy now? I really hope I am. Oh, I am. How could I not? When his eyes are this close to mine. And I could easily get lost in them. Because now I'm drowning in an ocean of emotions, mixed ones. Yet I'm only on the surface. I'm not allowed to go deeper to find what's under, yet I would very much like to go deeper, to know what's so deep inside, to know of the life I know nothing of. And maybe...maybe I could breathe underwater. Yet the ocean wouldn't answer you if you begged it to drown you. But, here, a little open door-

"Haven't you seen the woods? Would you love to?" He then cut off my thoughts and thus the silence.

What? "What?"

Keir.

"What?" She said with a confused angelic voice and picked her ginger brown hair behind her ear.

"I mean you haven't seen it around here, I know there might be a little traumatizing experience you had there, but well if you went with me I promise there is a lot of lovely stuff out there."

Her features changed quite quickly, and hope spread in me.

"Oh, I mean sure! I was just afraid something would eat me. You know I watch these documentaries where people literally get eaten by a lion. So you never know." She waited. "But I wouldn't worry about anything with you there." She gave a little chuckle.

"I'm pretty sure there aren't any lions around here but as you see."

"When?"

"Right now."

"You're kidding?"

"Not at all, let's go."

I can't touch her but maybe this will help. And hopefully, it could make up for my horrible attitude towards her.

My hands itched to touch her but...I can't. I fear it. Very much.

She jumped out of her chair and ran outside. And I followed.

When I got to her and began walking and she just followed. "Where are we going?" she asked impatiently.

"Just wait and watch." I smiled to myself.

I could feel her getting closer and closer as we walked and I could feel my heart thunder with every step she takes closer to me. Should I just tell her? But I wouldn't want to disturb her. Even if I could tell her we're already here.

"That's it? The end of a cliff?" she asked, looking at her feet.

"Look up," I advised.

When she did, I could hear her breath being taken away. And I wouldn't blame her.

The sun was clear, spreading its rays through the white clouds surrounding it, the gradient orange sky beamed through the big mountain that stood high on its face. It was an early hour, so the sun didn't really hurt even though it was just in front of us. A cool wind blew my hair away, and it tickled my face.

I looked over at her, her eyes were a small version of the sun when light struck them. I didn't know what to fancy more, the admiration that grew on her face or the view before me.

Somehow I chose to look at her, she caught me staring and turned her face away, and I felt a smile growing on my face.

"Feeling better?" I asked.

She nodded, "yes. It's so pretty,"

"It is." I didn't lift my eyes from her.

We talked about a lot of things, though silence was enough for us. It wasn't awkward it was just the kind of silence where you stay and feel, not listen.

We finally got up and went back to the house.

"I have to go now," she smiled. "thanks for breakfast, and for what you showed me. It...means a lot. And good luck waking these dumbheads on your own."

"I won't even attempt to." I smiled faintly.

"Goodbye," she said as she strode to the woods but stopped and turned to me "Wait! Have you seen my book?"

"Oh, yeah I almost forgot," I took it out of my black jacket's pocket and handed it to her, "here."

She blinked. "You read it? What- when?"

"I took it from you when you slept and stayed up all night reading it. I hope you don't mind."

"No, it's okay! I...hope you like it." She chuckled. "Anyway, I have to go." She turned to leave but came back again, "just so you know.. .Dylan gave me Your number and Alana's too." I nodded and smiled.

I'll actually kill him.

"Bye!" she said one last time and walked until there was nothing but trees to be seen.

What am I doing?

Why am I so desperate? Why am I getting close? I don't stand a chance. Am I asking for help? Or seeking her pity? And for what?

Was it Al's words last night?

"The girl is not a spy, Keir."

"What makes you so sure?" I'd asked

"I just know, it's obvious, she means no harm towards us."

"Oh, don't give me that look, did you see how scared she was when she saw us hunting? Or how tired she was when we raced or how happy she was when she threw that knife, or how she sleeps so peacefully with no worries. She's not a spy."

Was I waiting to hear those words?

What exactly did I want?

Just...

Teach me, Mirelle.

Chapter 8

Mirelle.

"Hello," I greeted Al as I approached the house.

"Hey." She mumbled, and quickly drew her head towards me for me to see the surprise in her eyes, but she looked back down just as quickly.

"I'm glad you grew to like me."

She waved me off with a hand, "where's the other dumbass?"

I already knew she spoke about Dylan. But what I don't know is why she thought I would knowm.

I was about to open my mouth when I heard Dylan's footsteps coming from the woods. He carried a deer on his shoulder. I turned my head to the other side away and gagged.

"Hey Mirelle," Dylan said as he came closer to Al, I still didn't look.

"How many times do I have to tell you not to go hunting alone? One time, Dylan, one time something is going to eat you and I won't even bother to come to visit your grave," she hissed.

Dylan's face paled, "I wasn't alone. Keir was with me."

"And why the hell didn't you take me with you?"

"You were asleep, and it wasn't that hard to catch a doe without you being here," Keir panted, approaching the house, with blood on his face.

I gagged again.

"Morons," she spat.

Keir shrugged. "You've called us worse." He turned his face towards me and must have noticed the sick impression I had. He snorted, "hello, Mirelle."

I waved my hand and didn't even attempt to look at his bloodied face. Why do they have to do this to me?

"You go to the merchants, Dylan. Get us a great deal."

Dylan nodded, and paced to the woods, with the doe still on his shoulder.

"Give me a moment," Keir said and walked inside the house.

"Are you okay?" Al asked sarcastically.

I scoffed and went to sit beside her. "I just can't...stand blood."

"Then you're at the wrong place," she murmured. And went back to her silence.

"You seem...disturbed?"

She didn't answer, just stared at the trees, like they were her only friend.

"You can tell me, you know. I won't tell anyone."

She didn't bother to look at me, "Baron, there are three days left."

I'll come again in fifteen days.

"Just who is Baron exactly?"

She raised her brows and her mouth flickered upwards, "Baron. Is a bastard."

"Yeah, I know. But what does he want?"

She leaned her back in the chair, "Three years ago, I got myself in a fight, he took me and threatened to kill my only friend if I didn't work with him in doing whatever the hell he tells me to do."

Dylan came and kept his distance from Al. Like he knew it wasn't easy for her to speak about that topic.

"He gave me a day in the week to do what I liked, but I wasn't supposed to talk to anyone or to ask for help." She clenched her fist. "One day, it was midnight, I was walking alone, thinking about how I hate everyone as usual, and I found that idiot crying like a divorced middle-aged Karen near a gas station," she waved a hand at Dylan. "And so I consoled him."

"You said you'll feed me to the dogs if I didn't stop crying."

"And it worked. Anyways, we talked, and I ended up telling him about my life, he just looked at me and told me to meet him again next week, and so I did.

"When we met at the same spot, it wasn't just Dylan, Keir was with him, I thought they were-" she paused and swallowed, "Keir told me to take him to Baron. At first, I didn't want to, but he insisted."

She stayed silent for a while, neither I nor Dylan dared to speak.

She said finally, "Keir and Baron made a deal, Keir takes me and Baron takes money, every month." That explains everything that happened that night.

"I'm sorry," I muttered.

"I don't need your pity." She faced me now, "I need you to do something."

"Anything," I breathed, and looked over Al's shoulder to find Dylan already gone.

She leaned in and reached my ear and whispered, "Keir won't tell me if he has the money or not, so if Baron comes I'll let him take me, and you, try to prevent Keir from coming again." She didn't let her eyes leave mine. "He can be stubborn as hell, but he thinks you could be trusted, which doesn't happen so often."

I opened my mouth to object but Keir came from the house, his hair damp and dripping, "I said no." No sign of the lovely face he gave me this morning, instead, he had what I call a hawk face; serious and scary. "End of discussion."

"You don't get to tell me what to do." She pointed a finger at him.

"And you don't get to make decisions by yourself." He snapped back at her.

"Keir is right Al, you can't just leave, we'll find something," Dylan said, coming out of the house with a new shirt.

"We were trying to find something for two years, and what happened? nothing!" She let loose of a breath, "just let me go."

"No!" Keir went on.

"Please stop," I let out. They all looked at me. "No need to fight." I shifted my gaze to Keir, "Keir, Do you have the money?"

He hesitated, "almost."

I nodded slowly and approached them, "I'll help you, I'll help you get the rest of the money, all of you."

"We only have three days," Dylan objected.

"I know, but rest won't be a problem." They blinked at me like I'm stupid. "When was the last time you got out of here? To have fun."

No answer.

"That's what I thought. C'mon, we're going outside."

No one moved, Keir's face paled.

"Just trust me, no one is going to bother you," I said to no one in particular, but Keir had a knowing look on his face.

"To where?" Dylan asked.

"Don't worry about that, just follow me."

Dylan stepped beside me, but Al and Keir didn't move.

"No one, no one will dare to even look at you, I promise." Al took an unsteady step towards me, and was beside me at last, Keir still didn't so much as blink.

So I took a step towards him, and he took a step back.

I don't know what's wrong. Every time someone comes near him he pushes them away. And that reminded me of the last time I tried to touch him; he flinched.

Is he scared?

"I won't let them, I won't let anyone come near you."

Still nothing.

"You can stay here if you want, that's okay, but we'll have fun."

He took one step to the front.

"You'll have fun, I promise, I'll get you all ice cream how about that?"

He took another step.

"Just tonight, and I'll help you with anything you ask, okay?"

My eyes never left him, I wanted him to see that I will never do anything to hurt him. I tried my best to show that I will never harm him, or allow it. I know better. And I guess he saw it because he nodded and moved to stand beside Al and Dylan.

I was happy, truly, and I didn't even try to hide it.

"Follow me." I smiled and stayed close to Keir, without touching him of course.

Keir.

I didn't get outside often, at least not for fun. And I didn't want to, I didn't dare.

And now I know why.

I couldn't stand it, my heart was pounding in my chest, my hands were shaking, I think I can't breathe properly. But I didn't let it show, I hid my hands inside my pockets and had a neutral face on.

But she knew.

She kept close, laughing around like there was nothing wrong.

"Mirelle, I know no one told you this, but we're all armed and if you tried to kidnap us we'll make you regret it," Al warned.

She giggled. "Like I'd dare"

"Good." Al pressed her lips in a line, though there was a pleasure in her eyes, I always knew that. And Dylan laughed, staying close to Mirelle's other side.

"Here it is," she announced. and we all looked at what she was looking at.

It was an...Amusement park.

Al snorted, "are you serious?"

"As serious as they get," she said with a wide smile as she took Dylan and Al's hands and ran to the gate.

She looked over her shoulders, "C'mon Keir." I had no choice but to follow. The park wasn't crowded anyway, which made it a little more comfortable.

They all strode to the roller coaster. An enormous one.

"Do you want to sit by my side? It's okay if you don't want to get on, but I've been here a couple of times and I absolutely love it," Mirelle invited.

"I would love that." And it was the truth.

"Great, Dylan and Al are already there." She didn't stand still for a second, she's got too much energy for me to process. I offered her a smile, which she returned with an even wider one.

And we got on the roller coaster, Dylan and Al were in the vehicle in front of us.

"Alana, you're crushing my spleen!" Dylan whined.

"Shut up Dylan! you don't even know where that is."

When it started to move, Dylan screamed but to his luck, Al was with him. She kicked him. "Close your mouth, you dumbass."

And then it was so fast I had to hold on tight to it, my knuckles turned white.

All of them were laughing, their hair flying on their faces. And that was all I wanted them to be, all I needed was to see them happy, so I laughed along, one from my heart.

We got down still laughing, then we rode the merry-go-round, and then we played darts, and of course, all of us won, except Mirelle for the first time, I instructed her carefully and she missed the second throw but aimed perfectly at the target for the third time.

An hour later Mirelle left us to go get ice cream. Dylan and Al went off somewhere, and now it was just us. when I walked I still tried to avoid everyone walking in the same way I did.

"Keir!" Mirelle called, I turned to find her on a bench patting the place beside her.

When I settled in she didn't lift her eyes from me, I tried to ignore it but she didn't stop.

"Keir?" she finally asked, "what's wrong?"

"What do you mean?" I asked even know I knew exactly what she means. No wonder she saw something wrong. all I do is show it.

"You know, you're kinda...distant." She shrugged.

"Nothing's wrong."

She didn't stop, instead, she went to touch my arm but of course, without thinking my body didn't allow it.

"I wouldn't have done it. I'm just showing you what I mean." She asserted.

I wasn't breathing.

"Tell me, Keir. Trust me." She brought her hand to her chest. "I promise you can."

I knew I shouldn't. I knew I'd probably regret this later. but I'm tired. I'm too tired and desperate that sometimes I dream of letting it out.

Her eyes were glittering with emotion. and I didn't understand why. why me and why would she care. No one had ever done this before.

So I did. so weakly and vulnerably.

I told her.

I swallowed my shaky voice but it still was clear, "When I was little, I really loved my father, but...he left. He simply just abandoned us. I felt like...like I wasn't worthy of any love anymore, I thought it was my fault and sometimes I thought I deserved it.

"I didn't know how he felt, if he was happy, or unsatisfied or if he hated us. I just constantly thought something was missing. My mother, of course, grieved. She didn't want me to know, but I did. It was so obvious on her face." My voice was foreign in my ears. and I didn't dare meet her eyes.

"Until two years after what happened, my uncle-" I could feel my face darken. "He convinced my mother he came to check on me and meet my dad, while he took me away to...beat me. She didn't know. She was at work thinking I was with dad.

"I don't know what was wrong with him, he just kept saying it was my fault that my father was in his state, I was young back then, I wanted to scream, I wanted to ask everyone for help but," I clenched my fist. "He said if I told anyone he'd do it harder next time. So for once, I tried to be useful.

"He looked into my eyes expecting to see a happy, innocent child. and deep down I knew she blamed herself for everything, so I shut up and took in all the beating. It hurt of course. But I... I kept quiet through every slap or kick or punch. I was grateful it was not her, because, while everyone was against her, she chose to be by my side and love me unconditionally."

I dragged my eyes to hers now.

"That's why I can't stand touching someone or being touched."

I scanned her face, waiting for the rejection, waiting for her to laugh me off and tell me that I was pathetic. Her face had just understanding in it. She watched me carefully. And I did the same.

"I didn't know." her voice coming out steady but raspy, "I didn't know, you fought that hard and that much." She swallowed. "You're a warrior, Keir. And I want to thank you, for telling me. It must be hard to express what hunts us. I'm with you, by your side to fight these monsters.

"I know how hideous they are, how they can keep you from sleeping at night, and how they keep you from living, I know them, Keir. But we're much stronger, these monsters were made to be defeated, they're just blind fools who have big mouths."

I frowned, not knowing how or why she'd tell me that. But I shoved it off. because I only felt one thing and I hadn't felt it in a while. relief.

"Thank you," I mumbled more to myself than to her.

She just nodded sternly.

After Dylan and Al came back, we stayed there for a while and finally got back home. Their smiles reached their eyes as they walked.

I approached Mirelle, "I want to thank you...for today, it's been a while since we laughed like that."

Her eyes softened. "You had fun?"

"Yes, a lot."

She smiled, "I'm glad." She reached for my arm but drew it back as she remembered.

But I extended my shaking hand and touched her shoulder and drew it back immediately.

She sucked in her breath, "I appreciate that." I gave her a tight smile in return.

We finally reached home, dragging our legs to move from the exhaustion, and rested on the couch.

"I need some water," Dylan said panting.

"Give me a minute." Mirelle stood and strode to the kitchen.

"Keir?" Dylan called. "I want to keep her. She feeds me."

"Grow up, Dylan." Al glared at him.

"At least she loves me and doesn't glare at me all the time!"

She was taking a lot of time in there, I figured something was wrong, so I stood up and followed her to the kitchen.

And I wish I didn't.

She was emptying the drawer I had the money in, on her other side the drawer that had Baron's messages was opened.

"What are you doing?" I breathed.

She lifted her head for me to find surprise and terror in her eyes.

Chapter 9

Mirelle.

I went to grab some water for all of them, but there was something wrong. it felt like someone had been here.

Two drawers were open.

I didn't even know what I was doing as my hands dragged me to the drawer, there was just money, but something must have been stolen so I got the money out and decided to tell Keir and the others.

"What are you doing?" Keir said so suddenly from the kitchen's door.

I lifted my eyes to see him standing utterly still, "I- nothing, I was about to come, you won't believe-"

"What. Are. You. Doing?" He repeated.

"I came here to get water, and I found those drawers open."

"Liar," he breathed, his face began to be red with rage. "I knew it."

"Keir, what do you mean-"

"Don't you dare." He snapped, pointing a finger at me. "You lied!"

"I'm not lying."

"Shut up." He looked at me with hatred, I didn't know was possible on his face, or at least I didn't imagine it. No sign of the pleasure he had before, "Dylan!"

Dylan and Alana came running, their faces searching ours with worry.

"Lock her up in a room," he said, not looking at me.

"Keir," Alana started.

"I said lock her up in a room!" he snapped.

"What- I don't understand. what have I done?"

"Don't speak. Don't even look at me," Keir said stepping away.

"Wait Keir, I'm not locking her up. What is wrong with you?" Dylan objected.

"Then get out," Keir answered rapidly.

"What?"

"It's either you do as I say or you get out."

"Do not speak to him like that!" I yelled, but Dylan was already heading outside.

"Shut up!" he shouted, "You deserve every bit of this. You really thought you could get us that easy?"

He looked at Al, "you heard me?"

Al took her dagger at stuck to my back with a shaking hand, and a pained look on her face.

I just moved, unable to take in what just happened, I let her drag me to whatever room they'll put me in, without saying a word.

Alana opened a door and there was just a simple room in there, so I stepped inside, sat on the floor and buried my face in my hands, and resting on my knees.

Alana still had that look on her face. She hesitated for a while, opened her mouth then closed again before she finally closed the door and a click sounded.

And they'd locked me up.

I haven't slept.

Didn't even try to move.

I just stared at the room while recalling everything he'd said.

Lair.Shut up.Don't look at me.You deserve it.

What have I done? Why am I a liar?

Do I really deserve that? Everything recalls the bad days at school when they used to call me all this bad stuff, and I'd sit in the same position, thinking if I was truly worthy of anything.

He hates me-

The door clicked at it was Dylan who stepped inside. "Hello," he greeted softly.

I didn't answer, just stared at him as he got inside.

He sat on the floor beside me, "What happened?" He asked after a long pause. Still quiet.

I rested my head on my knees.

"I'm sorry." He placed a hand on my back.

"He didn't even try to listen to me," I let out, with a shaky voice.

"I know," he whispered.

"Didn't try to listen to you." My throat tightened, "what have I done?" Tears ran down my face, but still, I didn't move it from my knees.

"It's the first time that I'd seen him like that," he said, "But please tell me what happened."

"I was in the kitchen to get you water, but it was clear that someone has been there. The drawers were opened so I was just checking

if something had been stolen, then he came in, accusing me of being a liar and that he knew it." I sobbed.

He stilled beside me.

"I'm sorry," he said, still rubbing my back, "I believe you."

"Thank you," I muttered.

He stayed beside me until I calmed down a little. "I knew I didn't say this earlier, but it was because...well, you know. But thank you, for last night. I've never been on a roller coaster in my life, and thank you for just being there, it was fun."

I nodded, didn't have the energy to even smile.

He sighed, "Al believes you too, you know."

I nodded again.

"He'll come to his senses, don't worry." He stood up, "I'll leave the door open for you, you can get outside if you want, and don't worry he's not here."

"I don't want to, and please close it I don't want to cause any trouble."

He hesitated, "then sleep, have some rest."

I won't, but I nodded anyway. He left and locked the door behind him.

Two hours passed, a shadow twirled under the door, it waited, as if hesitated to get in or not, but Keir called for Al and in a second the shadow disappeared.

I didn't do anything but glance at the clock they hung on the wall, and listen to myself breathe.

It was ten pm when the door clicked open again, but it wasn't only Dylan this time, Al was there too. They closed the door, carefully, and approached me.

Still, I didn't move.

Al had a tray with food and water in her hands. I didn't even notice or didn't have the time to notice I was hungry, I was busy...thinking.

"Eat up," she ordered.

I didn't move.

"Eat or I'll make you starve to death." I stilled.

"I told you to be nice," Dylan hissed.

She glared at him and rolled her eyes, but said, "eat...please."

I nodded but didn't move.

"Mirelle," she said, steadily.

How many times has she actually called me by my name?

"I want you to know that he did all of that because he thinks you're a spy."

What?

"It- he- when he first saw you, Keir and I thought you were a spy."

I don't know why am I even surprised.

"So we let you in, to keep an eye on you. But you appeared so...innocent, we believed you were no harm."

"So it wasn't out of love." I closed my eyes, "when you invited me to your party."

"Listen, there's nothing wrong with you, it's him. He barely trusts anyone." She waited, "but he trusted you."

But that's the problem, isn't it?

Trusted.

And it wasn't enough.

"He-"

"It's all him, him, him! Why are you all trying to defend him?" My voice grew louder, "If he's so perfect, then why not tell him I didn't do anything instead of praising him."

They exchanged looks.

"If I'm a liar to him, then he's just a freak." I continued, "how dare he lock me in a room? Who does he think he is? How dare he accuse me of being a liar and a spy in less than a second? And yet you choose to stay in his side!"

"We're not on his side!" Al yelled back.

I shut up.

"He hasn't been home since last night, and when he came back for once I tried to speak to him but he got himself a jacket and left again, I didn't have time to talk to him."

We stayed silent only listening to the rhythm of my loud noticeable breathing.

"Get out," I ordered.

"Mirelle," Dylan said.

"Get out. please," I repeated, "and lock the door, let him be happy." They stood there, not lifting their gaze from me. but eventually moved to the door.

Dylan was the first to leave the room but Alana waited and said, "I'll talk to him."

I didn't answer, mostly because I didn't care and because I didn't want to speak anymore. She left the room and locked the door.

I barely took two bites from the sandwich Alana placed on the tray.

Did Jenny miss me? I hope she didn't write my story yet. I miss my parents.

An hour or so passed and I felt someone open the house door. I could feel it coming inside.

I didn't move.

It waited just in front of my door, and I could see the shadows lingering under the door.

It was-

I knew precisely who that was. And it wasn't Dylan or Alana. But I didn't care, didn't even try to wait for him to open the door. I just waited, feeling him standing there, with his too stiff shoulders.

Did he even think of what he said?

Did he even think even if it was for a moment that maybe, I wasn't going to hurt them after all?

Does he blame himself? Because if not I'd gladly do it for him.

So I stood up and went to the door.

Chapter 10

Keir.

She opened the door with such ferocity, I stumbled back a few steps. But then she came in sight, her hazel eyes full of exhaustion.

I sucked in my breath.

She eyed me, with such rage, and I did the same, but with utter numbness.

She brought it upon herself, that wasn't my fault, that exhaustion, it was her fault.

But her eyes said otherwise.

Lies. Just lies.

Someone make this stop.

Don't look at me.Shut up.Liar.

She did this, she tried to rob us, and she tried to hurt-

I'm tired.

"You. Are. A. Piece. Of. Shit," she spat, slowly.

And she shut the door in my face. I still stood there, not knowing what got me here in the first place. Then decided to leave.

Dylan.

Get out I'd said. I was full of anger and wrath, and for what? So I walked to Dylan's room and knocked.

No one answered.

I knocked again.

He opened the door. From what it seemed, he had been sleeping, as he rubbed his eyes and stood before me. He blinked as if not believing it was me.

"What?" he spoke at last.

"I'm sorry," I answered, "I was angry."

"Don't try to justify it."

"I'm not." I sighed, "I'm just sorry, really sorry."

He looked me up and down, but said, "it's alright. Did you apologize to her too?"

I knew who he meant. "No. And I won't." I folded my arms over my chest weakly.

"Why?"

"Because she's-"

"Because she's what, Keir? Let me just remind you of how many people put the effort to make us just simply smile, oh yes, no one! and yet the first one who tries to get closer, you do what? You accuse her of being a spy and a lair."

He doesn't see it, none of them do, they fell right into her trap without even trying to be cautious.

Al seemed to be awakened by Dylan's loud voice. "What's wrong?" she asked to no one in particular, but her eyes seemed to focus on me as she took in my presence.

"You locked her in a room! Are you insane?" Dylan continued anyways.

Why does nobody understand? "No, I'm not, and again I'm not apologizing to her, I wasn't doing that to break your so gentle hearts, I was protecting you. She is danger, and I won't just let her wander around the house like there's nothing. If there was a one percent chance that she's a harm I wouldn't have hesitated to do what I did." I glared. But did I mean it?

Yes. Of course, I did.

"What's your proof then?" Al said. "Why are you so sure she's with Baron?"

"I saw her," I answered back.

"We all did, and yet we trust her enough to tell that she hasn't done anything."

I lost it. "Half the money is gone! And she was standing right there. So tell me, Al, what the hell are we supposed to do in two days?"

Their eyes widened. "The money's gone?" she breathed.

"Yes."

They were all so quiet. Just looking at me. I realized they were waiting for an answer.

"Rest for today, we wake up tomorrow morning. Grab the daggers and the ropes, we'll try our best, and won't stop until dawn." They nodded, grieve and disappointment on both their faces.

I was just about to leave when Al said, "I still believe her, she didn't do it, Keir."

"Well I don't," I said and left.

Idiots, both of them were idiots.

I tried, really tried, with all my power to trust her. I let her in and showed her, I showed her the mess, the chaos. I thought she understood, I thought it was okay, I thought she would help me. I wanted her to stay, to show us the life she lived, to laugh at everything as she does, and I wanted her to see, to see us, what life has made of us and love it. All of it.

But she had to come and mess up everything.

I wanted to believe her so badly.I wish my eyes could lie, so I'd believe her.

But maybe I was stupid to keep hoping.

I was furious that night. I'd wanted to look into her eyes again and see once again that look she gave me to make me trust her. But it wasn't there, it was only her taking the money for whatever purposes.

So I slid into the tent that I set, a few minutes away from the house, I wanted to get away from all of them, and from her.

As I was closing my tent zip I heard footsteps, but I'm used to these anyways. and whatever is there either to kill me or eat me will look at me and probably feel sorry, so I stayed inside.

It's enough work for today, I'll wake up early and continue to hunt.

I tried to close my eyes and summon sleep, but it never came.

you are a piece of shit.

very well then.

Mirelle.

I didn't know what to do all night, so for once I got up to my feet. They hurt, of course, and walked to the desk that was facing the bed. I opened a drawer. It was empty. I mean what did I expect? So I opened the one beneath it.

I found a notebook.

it seemed old from the yellowness of its papers and the damaged cover. But what else do I do? I took the notebook to the bed, finally giving my body some rest, and turned to the first page.

Sherlock Holmes would have done it. Even if he was the reason I'm here right now. They could be murderers for all I know, and they could write the victim's names here. But anyway, I started reading

Mother, you cry like rain.but clouds don't hide their pain.hold me and cry, let me touch your scars.I could feel them from a mile away,but all I see is the sun in your face.

I turned the page, carefully.

Why promise you'll stay when you'll fade away?why say you care when I'm easily replaced?shall I be a flower and you shall be a petal.To leave and fall when we grow old.But I assume, even if we didn't grow,time wasn't our ally anyway.

I hopped to the half of the notebook.

every scratch you laid upon me may be invisible now.but I can hear them.screaming, asking for helpor perhaps it's just me.

I started reading the last few pages.

I cannot stand touching. I fear it's him.but you held me,without even touching me.

Keir.

Keir wrote that.

I was going to continue reading, but someone knocked on the door, so I shoved the notebook back in the drawer and glanced at the clock, it was five am.

"Come in," I said.

It was Keir.

I didn't speak, didn't want to, so I just waited for him to say what he has to say.

"Sit down. On the bed." He warned.

"No."

"Why?"

"Because I can do whatever I wish."

He gave me a challenging look. but I didn't move an inch. "Where's the money?" he asked, still giving me that look.

"What money?"

"Don't play stupid." He raised his finger at me.

"Oh, put that stupid figure down and say what you want to say and get on with it."

"In the drawer, the money you took from the drawer."

I looked at him up and down. " I said this once and I'll say it again, I have no intention in taking your money, and that damn drawer was open when I got in."

"Then why not tell me the same moment you saw it? Why dig your hand in the drawer and even take the money out of it?"

"I- I don't know. I just did, but I was going to tell you."

"Just what did he send you for exactly?" he asked, frowning.

"Nothing! He didn't send me, and I didn't do anything."

"Quit lying!"

"I'm not lying. Why do you keep saying that?" At that point, my hands were shaking? I hate being yelled at.

"You lied when you said you were lost that night in the woods. Why wouldn't you be lying now?"

I felt my eyes burn, but I won't allow myself to cry. "Because I was scared."

"Of what?" he pressed.

I'm truly tired of this.

"Of you," I whispered. Shutting my eyes tight.

No. I will not just stand there and let that douche bag make me cry. I am power. where the hell was my confidence?

Finally, he shut up.

Dylan and Alana came running to the room.

they must have seen my panic on my face because Dylan asked, "what's wrong?"

"Nothing," I said. "I want to call my parents."

"I'll call them," Keir said, his eyes like the hawk.

I rolled my eyes. "Fine."

He drew his phone from his jacket's pocket, I took it from him, and dialed my mother's phone number and gave it back to him, he turned on the speaker's mode.

"Hello?" Keir said.

"Hello," my mother answered, she sounded...exhausted.

"Is this Mrs...." Keir glanced at me in question.

"Austin," I whispered, but she didn't seem to hear my voice.

"Mrs. Austin?"

"Yes."

"I'm- I have your daughter."

She didn't speak. "Anything. Demand anything and I'll give it to you, just don't hurt her, please." I can sense the change in her voice, she was sobbing.

"I don't want anything, and to assure you, she's not here to be harmed. I would never," he whispered the last part, his eyes gazing into nothing.

So Dylan snatched the phone from Keir's hand. "Hello ma'am, I know it's a bit hard to understand what's going on right now. But don't worry about your daughter, she is just fine, in fact, you can call her now, but just don't be worried, she's in good hands." He glanced softly at me, with a slight smile.

I smile right back, swallowing away the tears.

"I'm sure she's even told you about us, or at least I wish we were good company enough that she did. Which I do not doubt that we are, though."

Al let out a sigh of disappointment.

"We're her...friends. She's safe," he said so reassuringly, I would be convinced.

"You're the friends from the party?" my mom mumbled.

"Yes," Keir said instead, getting ahold of himself again.

"I need to come to see her, please."

"That's not possible."

"Please." She pleaded.

"You heard her! Let her do what she wants." I yelled at him.

Keir eyed me and considered. "Fine." He sighed.

"I'll call you later to tell you how to come here, but we'll meet at twelve."

"Let me speak to her." He looked at me over his brow.

"I'm okay mom, I'm okay," I said, still sobbing.

She let out a sigh of relief, "I'll come with your father."

"You're very welcome," Dylan said softly.

"Thank you," she whispered and hung up.

We stayed silent.

Then Keir broke it, "We get to work now, then come meet her parents." They both nodded and walked out of the room. Keir right behind them, he closed the door but he didn't lock it.

Now it was just me.

I waited for all of them to leave the house and continued reading in Keir's notebook. I waited till they all came back, but stayed inside the room, they all showered and dressed well.

And Dylan came to tell me that I can come out now. I did, and we all waited for my parent's arrival.

They came in sight. The air blowing my mom's light brown hair and my dad's blond hair. They walked inside the house and my mother hugged me tightly, I realized I missed it. My dad just scanned me up and down to check if I was hurt.

Keir cleared his throat. "You can sit down."

They sat beside each other, I always admired their love for each other. Al didn't lift her eyes from them.

"Now that we're all here, I can make my point."

They nodded.

"Your daughter is under suspicion of being a spy who works with someone- a bad guy."

They scanned him, frowning. "Excuse me," my dad said, eventually.

"Your daughter-"

"Are you serious?" my dad asked.

"Yes, I am," Keir answered, and I knew he was losing his temper.

My dad snorts. "She can barely open a can of soda."

Keir's face didn't move an inch.

"Why?" mom asked. "What happened?"

"She's-" he looked at my mom deeply and then at me, "I can't tell you."

"When can she come again?" my mom asked with a low voice.

"Till it's been confirmed otherwise."

My mom nodded. "You won't hurt her, will you?"

Keir lifted his chin high, "No. I won't."

What's wrong with her? Normally she's chill, why is she so...stiff?

"How old are you?" my dad asked, all of them.

"Nineteen," Keir answered, "Dylan is seventeen, and Alana is nineteen."

"What do you do for a living?"

"Murder." Dylan snorted, and Al glared at him. Both my parents went still.

Keir glared at him for that too.

"We-" I've never seen him in such loss of words. Was he embarrassed? Was the Keir embarrassed?

"They hunt," I said, in their places. "They're really good hunters."

My dad seemed impressed. "Such a talent for someone as young as you."

It was now that Keir said in a steady voice, "We have to."

My dad cleared his throat, "Well it was nice to meet you, Kevin-"

Mom nudged him with an elbow, "it's Keir."

"It's nice to meet you, Keir, and the other lads as well, but unfortunately I have to take her back." My dad said.

"We're not asking for her hand in marriage." Al glared.

"No," Keir said still with that bored face.

My dad was about to stand up, but mom held his arm tightly and gave him the look.

He sat back down.

"We understand, Keir," my mom said, standing up with my dad slowly. "Please, take care making decisions." She looked at him, with no sarcasm as usual. Just pure seriousness. He nodded.

We followed them out of the house. My mother looked at me one last time. Like she was dying to talk to me. And I only wanted to hug her. She strode to the woods clutching tightly to dad's arm. Ten minutes later and they left.

Keir turned to say something to me. But...he had no time.

Men scattered around the house, A lot of them. All of them were the size of the freaking Titanic.

And in the middle stood the bastard Baron.

"Well hello there Keir," Baron greeted.

Keir took a step back, Dylan stepped right in front of me, and Alana stood behind me. They didn't want him to see me.

"Where's my money? Let me guess, you don't have it."

They didn't speak. Didn't even move. I'm not sure they're breathing.

"Well guess what, I do happen to change my mind," he continued.

"I'm not taking her," he said, and I feel Alana stiffen behind me. "I'm taking you instead."

No.

"After all, you're much more useful to me than her."

No!

"I have half of the money," he said shakily. "And a little more."

Baron- the bastard frowned, "but that's not our deal, is it?"

"You took the money," he said to Baron but looked at me, such hate like fire.

Baron looked at the same way Keir direction looking.

And...He laughed.

What the hell is wrong with this psycho?

"You think it's her? I would hate to break it to you, but no, it's not her. You see, I did take the money."

Keir Stilled as a stone.

Suck it, Keir.

"Who then? Who did it?" he asked so quietly.

Baron clicked his fingers, one of his men came out of the shadows and shoved her to the ground.

She lifted her head from the ground.

It was-

No.

Not her.

Not again.

"Why?" I asked Jenny, my question coming out not more than a whisper, but she heard it.

Tears slid on her cheeks, and I was pretty sure I felt mine do the same. "I didn't have a choice." She sobbed. "He made me do it."

I felt like there was a layer on my heart, squeezing it, so it could hurt more than it already does. But what do I do except act like it doesn't matter? It does.

"Enough of this already!" he groaned, "get him," he said to his men. They immediately strode to Keir.

And I found my legs do the same, but Dylan held my wrist too tight. "Stay here," he whispered to my ear and motioned to Alana as they both ran.

They took out their daggers and fought. They fought so hard I could watch them do it for hours. Keir tookout his dagger and joined them as well.

I didn't know what to do.

Jenny was on the floor.

They wanted Keir.

And my friends were in danger.

God, help us.

I ran to Jenny and helped her on her feet. "Get inside," I told her. She nodded with fear in her eyes and ran to the house.

Someone was lurking at Keir from his back, I didn't know what to do but I did what I remembered. I went and grabbed his foot and pulled it, the guy stumbled and fell.

Ninja Turtles would be proud.

I kicked his back hoping to keep him down. But it's like I never did anything. the guy rose easily. He wasn't really happy.

He clenched his fist and walked towards me and I took a step back.

Here it is. A good death with Jenny even here to watch. She would write it all down. If she still cared.

The guy was fast, he took my wrist and pushed my whole body To to a tree, I fell. I tried to rise but the guy was already stepping on my leg. And he was damn strong. He was about to reach for me again when he held his abdomen and fell.

Keir was standing behind him was a bloodied knife.

"Can you stand up?" he asked softly. Concern filled his eyes along with...guilt.

As he should.

"Yes."

"Get inside."

I narrowed my eyes at him. "No."

A guy came to Keir with a knife in his hand but Keir twisted his arm behind his back and kicked his hand so he dropped his knife and stabbed him in the shoulder, and then in the stomach.

"Get inside!" he shouted, as more people ran to him.

"No!" I shouted back.

I took the knife from the guy on the ground and ran.

But slowed when I approached Baron, he was standing, watching everything, and looked like he was losing his temper.

What the hell am I doing? I was behind a tree, so close to him.

Screw this.

I came out of the trees, he didn't have time to look at me as I stabbed the knife through his hand. I never did this to anyone. It was just terrifying. My hands shook, and I couldn't breathe, I could hear my heart in my ears.

The knife was in Baron's hand. And there was blood on both our hands.

I hate blood.

So I ran, as away from him as I could. I saw Keir's eyes widen at what I did, he didn't see the man behind him.

I wanted to warn him, I wanted to scream at him, but when I opened my mouth no voice came out.

I was going to collapse.

The man wrapped his arms around Keir, and I could see his face grow pale at the touch.

Stop.

A car was stopped right beside him, the man shoved Keir in the car. Keir still fought against them.

The other men took the dead and injured to the car too.

I saw Dylan and Alana running to the car, blood on their faces, but the car was much faster and all the men disappeared.

And that was when it all came black.

Chapter 11

Mirelle.

I woke up on a bed, every part of my body hurts. My eyes cleared out and I saw Dylan standing beside the bed, Alana resting her face in her palms. It took me a while to remember what actually happened last night.

I sat right up. "They took him!" I was panting, "we can't leave him there!"

Dylan patted my back at set me back to bed, "I know," he whispered.

"Please, Dylan. We can't just sit here and do nothing." I struggled as I fought his grip, and Alana just buried her face between her palms even more.

"We won't," he said painfully. And I'd say he didn't sleep all night from the redness and exhaustion of his eyes.

I tried to stand up but Dylan held me down. "You shouldn't be moving-"

"I'll be fine." I stood up, and my head spun and I fell back to the bed.

"Please." I began to sob, "they could hurt him." I recalled every word Keir said about his uncle.

"Calm down." Dylan's voice came out shaky.

I got back up slowly, still panting. I repeated, "they could hurt him." Alana's chair shook from across the room.

"We will help him, we'll come for him, I promise," he said. It was just when he said that, that I calmed down. A little.

No one spoke, no one had the energy to.

"Thank you for helping," Dylan said at last. He didn't lift his eyes from the floor. I ignored him. My mind was too busy thinking about how to get to Keir.

Dylan handed me a glass of water, and I drank it and sat up straight. "Alana," I said, my voice steady. She didn't try to look at me or answer.

"I need your help," I declare. "Help me, get him back."

She still didn't move.

"Please."

"You'll fail," she said finally, her voice raspy.

"I don't care," I said, "help me, even if it was a one-present chance. I'll take it."

I rose from the bed, and Dylan was beside me as I approached her. I sat down beside her chair. "What do you want?" she asked weakly.

"You've been there, haven't you?"

She nodded, her eyes just dark and empty I'm scared for her.

"You know it there?"

"Yes."

There was hope, there is always hope. I know that.

"I need a full description of the place," I tell her.

"You won't be able to cross the guards," she mumbled.

"Are there any other doors then? Anything that leads inside without being seen."

"I think so-"

I didn't let her finish as I pulled her up to her feet and took Dylan's arm and led them out of the room. They didn't argue. But as I lead them to the table, I come face to face with Jenny.

She stares at me, and I do the same. Her eyes were sore and red. She burst out crying, I mean hysterically crying.

"I'm sorry." She manages and falls to her knees. I let go of Dylan and Al's hands and kneel beside her.

"He threatened to hurt you and I didn't know what to do," she sobbed. "I didn't want to do it." She lifts her eyes to Al and Dylan. "Please forgive me."

"He's a bastard," Al let out.

"I took the money. I stole It. All of it." She takes a deep breath in, "and I didn't know what to do."

"Jenny," I say, as I reach for her. "It's not your fault. Don't blame yourself. You couldn't have done anything."

She simply nods.

"It's okay." I pat her back. "It's over. Are you hurt?"

She shook her head but I knew she fell hard when the so-called man threw her to the ground.

"Get up with me." I held her hand, gently. She stands with me. And I can't help but let out a sigh of relief.

"Help us, help us bring him back," I told her.

Her brown eyes shifted to mine. "Really?"

"We need help," Dylan came closer, putting a hand on her shoulder.

She nodded quickly, "Yes. Yes, please." So I led them all to the table. Everyone took their places, and I inhaled before I took my seat and started.

"Jenny, have you been there? At Baron's building?" I ask as gently as possible.

She silently nodded, she looked as white as a paper.

"So now, Jenny and Alana are the only ones who've been there, do you know the place there? And where everything is?"

"Yes," they say at the same time.

"I need a paper," I said, and Dylan got up and got me a stack of paper and some pencils.

"Can you and Jenny draw everything in the building on the paper?"

"Like a map?" Al asked with no emotion on her face, but I saw hope glimmering in her eyes, even if it was a little bit.

"Yes," I answered.

"I can try, though I may not remember some details."

"I can help you," Jenny mumbled. Alana nodded and took the pencils and a piece of paper.

She drew everything, with a few notes from Jenny.

"There are six floors in the building, the first one is a reception with the annoying brat of a secretary sitting there," Al explained.

"Second one is where all of his useless men work in their offices," she paused, "I was locked in an empty room there." Her eyes darkened.

"Third floor is the office of the excuse of human bein-"

"Okay, Alana we get it, you hate them all," I interrupted her.

She glared at me and sighed. "Baron's office is on the third floor along with his room that extends from his office, where he keeps some weapons," she continued.

"Fourth floor, there are the cells, and also a security room where they watch what's going on on the cameras and all, both are separated with a wall.

"Fifth floor, there is the weaponry and a room where they make his stupid calls-"

"We get it," I stopped her again.

"And there's also a room where his guys sit and drink.

"The sixth floor is just a bar."

"Can you point out where are the guards on the map?" I asked and when she did, I almost lost a bit of my hope. The guards were everywhere. "Would they let me into the bar?"

She shrugged, "If they knew you, which I don't think they do."

"Wait. If you want to get to the bar, how would you do that if it's on the last floor?" Dylan frowns.

"It's clear enough that I drew stairs in the outside back of the building that leads to the bar, you just needed to use your eyes."

"It looks like a dead worm."

Al glared at him. Of course.

"Do they know who Dylan is?" I asked. "The guards?"

"I don't think so."

"What about Jenny?"

"I think they do, but briefly," Jenny said quietly.

We argued about everything that could work out in our favor, and everything they couldn't. Most of it was Alana whining about how much of a bastard Baron is and me trying to calm her down with Dylan thinking he's funny. He is, but it's not the time for this.

Al told us about everyone that works there, whom we might have a good chance of talking to, and who's well, not nice.

I took a deep breath. "So here's what we're going to do." I made sure everyone is paying attention. "Jenny, you're going there again."

She stilled.

"You're not seeing Baron, don't worry." Her shoulder relaxed. "You're going inside the building, you'll be trying to get close to all the guards in the building. I want them all to trust you."

She nodded.

"And while you're there...try to find where Keir is, can you do that?" I know it was nearly impossible but there's nothing better to do than beating the odds.

She swallowed, "I'll try my best."

Dylan's concern showed on his face. "How long will she be doing this?"

"A week," I answered.

"You're leaving Keir there for a week?" Al stood her eyes were like a predator's.

"I don't think it could be any sooner," I swallowed, dreading it myself. Al kept glaring at me but eventually sighed and sat down slowly.

"You won't come back till the fourth day to tell us where Keir is and everything you did. Make sure no one follows you. If you didn't return that's how we know something is wrong." I continue to Jenny.

"What do I do with the guards?" She asked.

Before I could answer Alana did it herself. "The guards were always kind. They were just doing their jobs because they didn't have any other chance to do anything else. They were something far from the thugs in the building. They were friends."

Jenny nodded and I smiled at her, hoping she'd smile back, which she weakly did.

"Now rest today, go tomorrow."

"No." She stood, "I'm going now, he helped you, all of you. Now it's my turn."

"Jenny you-"

"It's the least I could do anyways. End of discussion," she said, looking at her feet.

I blinked at her, and then ran and hugged her tightly. She was always this way. Brave and loyal. And me sending her back there makes me hate myself but...I can't think of any other way that won't get us killed.

"I'm sorry you had to go through all of that, it wasn't your fault."

She patted my back and stood up to get to work, she said the building is an hour away from here, so I wished her luck, and we all did.

Keir.

"So it's simply your choice," Baron standing outside the cell that he put me in. He kept glancing at the bandage on his wrist.

I didn't answer.

"You know it's your little friends' lives that are on the line, right?" I still didn't speak, just stared numbly at the ropes tying me to the dirty, greasy chair.

"Well you'll have to speak or it won't go as you wish, Keir." I didn't even bother to lift my face from the floor.

Baron sighed and motioned to someone, I heard the cell's door crack open and a man stood right in front of my chair that I was tied to.

"For the last time, boy. Do as I tell you," Baron said in a warning tone.

Still, I said nothing.

That was when I felt my face burn with pain, I could feel the blood on it already.

"Answer, Keir!" he warned.

When I didn't, the guy threw another punch and the blood just kept dripping down my face.

He kept asking me to join him in his work, but I didn't speak. I won't.

The guy in front of me kept punching me until there was no place on my face, so he kicked me in the gut.

"If you continue rejecting my offer, I'll hurt your friends right in front of your eyes without hesitation, and it will be your fault," he spat. The man kicked me again before they both left.

And the history repeated itself.

I tried to ignore my shaking hurt body as I threw my head back.

"You think you're the victim now don't you?" My uncle's voice echoes in the whole house. And I could smell the alcohol on him.

"Come here you little-," he cursed as he held me tightly I couldn't move or breathe. "He gets home every day drunk."

Tears filled my eyes.

"And you know the only thing he speaks of?" I shook my head. "You. You did this to him!" he spat.

It was my fault.

"Now, Sit on the floor," he demanded.

It was a mistake to say no. I feared it. Yet somehow, "Please." I shook hard as I spoke.

"Please? I'll show you what please does."

He kicked my back so hard my face hit the floor.

He took my face between his big hands, and then punched me in the gut. And kicked me.

"Please, it hurts!" I sobbed.

"It hurts? And what you did, that didn't hurt your father? You deserve it."

He kicked me one last time before he said, "get up."

"I can't," I still sobbed.

He grabbed my shoulder and lifted me harshly. "One word about this to your mother, and I'll burn your finger. Tell her you fell on your back."

I was still crying but I nodded.

It's all under my clothes so it wouldn't be seen. It won't be a problem to hide it from my mother.

What's begging going to do?

Nothing. Absolutely nothing. And neither will speaking. I deserve this. Every single moment of it.

I locked her in a room and accused her without even listening. Let me get what I deserve. I'm stupid for even thinking they'll come for me.

Why would they? Why did she fight for me like I didn't do anything? Why did they all fight? Why didn't they just let me go?

Because now I'll just sit here, make myself recall everything I did. And I'll let him do whatever he wants with me. I will just pray they run away from the house, and never come back. I'll pray that they're all fine. That she's fine.

And I'll get whatever bruises he gives me and hide it.

But this time, I'll really think about what I did.

Chapter 12

Mirelle.

It's been a week since Keir has been taken.

Jenny's spent seven days there trying to gain the guard's trust. I didn't think it'd work, I thought they'd just go tell Baron.

Turns out Jenny is a way better friend than I thought.

She succeeded in disabling the security cameras there as I instructed, and when she came back she had a look on her face that I didn't see so often, "Keir's in the cells," Jenny said. "It was hard to look at him for a long time; he had blood all over his body." But I'm coming for him, we all are.

As Jenny leads us through the woods, Dylan doesn't stop his what-ifs about our failure, once he even said, "what if Keir refused to come with us because he now has a wife and is happy with his life." or, "what if Baron's toilet was dirty and he made us clean it for him as a punishment."

But Al just threatens to punch him in the face and make him spit his teeth. That keeps him quiet. for a while.

And now he's complaining about not having enough food when he pretty much ate half of the food alone that morning.

I think I will punch him.

And finally...here we are, standing in front of the bastard's building. And as our plan, we move.

Jenny, Dylan, and I take the stairs to the sixth floor which is the bar. Somehow, they let us in immediately after seeing Jenny.

Good.

She leads us out of the bar quickly and opens another door that leads to the stairs of the fifth floor. Jenny tries her best to show her face under the hood of her jacket. And in return, she's greeted by the guards with wide smiles.

And then on the fourth floor, The cells.

Alana, to her credit, was able to get inside the building from the main entrance and made her way up to the fourth floor without anyone talking to her. This may be because she was well covered and played the 'I'm Sara Toshi and I came to see Baron -whoever that was- correctly. Or she just gave them one of her glares that probably sent them running.

For all we know, here she is in front of the guards of the cells. "Long time no see, Jeff." Her voice came out deeper than it usually sounded. It was the thing between hate and longing, or maybe neither. I wouldn't know. "Bet you were looking for me for a while."

Jeff's eyes widened, then he smirked. "I bet Baron would love to see you, Alana Li."

We didn't have time to waste, although I would love to sit there and listen to them fighting, I bet Alana would win though.

We descended the stairs as slowly as we can, following Alana's rules on how to not make a sound. But obviously, Dylan forgot that because he was busy eating when she was talking.

I promise I'll punch him.

To our luck no one listened or even looked at us; they were busy with Alana.

We open the door to the cell as planned. Not locked, Jenny made sure. The place inside was horrific. blood was everywhere, and I nearly puked. the cells were empty, and all of them were muddy and just disgusting.

And then Keir came in sight. That hard pressure that occupied my heart for a week was finally gone.

Dylan and Jenny were walking fast, but somehow I felt myself going faster.

Don't say it. Don't say it. Don't say-

"I have come for you, my love!" I announced, but he didn't even flinch.

He didn't move, he just sat there on that chair looking at the floor. My heart starts pounding and I swallowed as we approach him.

I saw his face. His face had dried blood on it, his eyes were swollen and purple, his shirt was stained with blood, and he wasn't moving. There was too, too much blood.

My head began to spin.

Jenny handed us the key to the cell which she took from the guards when they were drunk. I opened his cell instantly. I put my finger under his nose to check if he's breathing.

Thank God. He is.

"Keir." I try to wake him up. He doesn't move.

"He's passed out, and we don't have time," Dylan said, cutting the ropes that tied Keir with his dagger.

Jenny took her jacket off and put it on Keir, then she put on the hood for him.

Dylan took Keir's arm and warped it around his neck. "Can you do that?" he asked me. I took Keir's other arm and put it around my shoulder. I tried to ignore the blood as we both stood up and carried Keir.

That idiot was heavy.

"Now go, get out the building. Try as hard as you can to let him stand and cover his face," she advised. "I don't think Alana could hold the guards any longer, so go."

We nodded and strode to the stairs, carrying Keir on both our shoulders. As we ascended the stairs to the fifth floor the guards looked at us. My breath was stuck in my throat. But Dylan and I tried to balance Keir as much as we could to make it seem like it's Jenny.

The guards shrugged and turned to what they were doing.

Great, this might actually work.

We got to the bar. No one looked at us there. We walked to the opposite way of the room until we came face to face with the exit of the bar. We stood in front of the stairs that will descend us.

It was so high the trees seemed like the size of ants, and the stairs seemed endless from here. It's okay. I tell myself. We made it this far.

"Uh, Mirelle?" Dylan started. "I know it's a good thing we went through all of this and all but if at some point we fall from I-don't know-how-many-thousand steps and break our necks it's Keir's fault."

"It sure is," I agreed.

We took the first step. Clinging tightly to Keir.

When we reached half the steps, we could see Alana and Jenny getting out of the main entrance and walking towards the woods. Their eyes met ours with the widest smiles.

Dylan chuckled, "We made it!" he exclaimed. "We actually made it!"

I laughed along, feeling the relief in my chest. "We did. But we have to keep going or else we're all going to die."

Dylan still laughed but took another step. And eventually, we were all on down there. All of us.

We didn't waste our time celebrating but carried Keir through the woods until we arrived at the house. Dylan opened Keir's room and we laid him on his bed.

I hope he knows that my back hurts from carrying his heavy horrible body.

Alana runs to the kitchen and grabs a wet towel and massaged his face with it, also wiping the blood.

"He needs medical attention, does someone knows a doctor?" I said, internally panicking.

"My older brother," Alana said firmly, "I'll call him." And she ran to get her phone.

Alana's older brother looked exactly like her, the soft black hair, the brown eyes, the freckle on the left cheek, even the glare. I didn't hear what he said though, All I know is that Keir is waking up soon, and I'm going to scold the thing out of him when he does.

I didn't realize how worried I grew, I didn't sleep these nights, thinking about how they'd hurt him, how he is. I was supposed to be mad at him, I even made a promise to myself that I'd slap him in his sleep, and then add cinnamon in his apple juice because he told me he hated it.

And then slap him again. That's all for yelling at me nonsense.

Just wake up Keir, wake up.

Al's brother left and Jenny left after I thanked them both a hundred times, and now it was just the four of us in Keir's room.

Nice room though-

Keir's eyes fluttered open. He blinked at the ceiling couple of times, as if not believing he's here.

Dylan was beside him in a moment, Al stood a step away and I stood from the chair I sat on. "Keir, you were going to kill us-" Dylan started and Al glared at him.

Keir's eyes only fell on me. "Why?" His voice came out not more than a whisper.

"You know why." I showed him the look I gave him that day when we went to the park. He never took his eyes away. I would never hurt you. Or allow it.

"I wouldn't miss the opportunity to chide you, and also remind you how much of an idiot you are," I said instead.

His eyes were still pierced on me scanning every part of me, his brows frowned as if just seeing me hurts him.

He swallowed, "I'm sorry, I'm truly sorry." He struggled to sit, but his whole body hurts, obviously.

"Don't Move, you should rest," I said, with a boring look. "I'll see if I'll forgive you or not." I picked at my nails. I'm a woman, and I can do whatever I like., including torturing Keir.

He nodded and leaned his back on the bed again.

The room was quiet for a while. Then Dylan decided to speak, "Keir, you won't believe what we did-"

"I said leave him for now!" Alana snapped. But Dylan brushed her off and continued anyways. Her nose flared but she took my hands and left the room.

She stood in front of me, she stared at me as I'm looking at her. She looked like she was struggling to speak. "Thank You," she said with a tight voice. "For bringing him back, we would have never done it without you."

I nodded. "It's okay."

She hesitated. "Do you hate him?"

I shook my head. "I never hated Keir. I like him, and I even understand why he did all of that, it's just that- he didn't try to listen. Neither to you nor to me, even though he knew I'd never do such a thing." She just eyed me, from head to toe.

Then she threw herself at me. At first, I thought she was going to attack me or something, but she wrapped her arms around me and drew me closer.

"Thank you," she repeated.

I patted her back and hugged her back.

Who knew she could actually hug someone. this wild.

We let go in an awkward way and entered Keir's room again.

Dylan, of course, was still talking. Keir held a pillow over his head to cover his ears but that didn't bother Dylan in the slightest.

He removed the pillow when Dylan finally shut up, by one of Alana's threats, might I add.

He looked at me, slowly, "thank you," he said softly, "all of you."

"We nearly got killed, Keir, But we guessed we liked you enough to risk it, so you're welcome," Dylan said. Alana and I nodded in agreement.

He rested his head back on the pillow and closed his eyes tightly. I found my hand itching to trace the wounds on his face, and see if they would disappear if only I-

No.

I don't care what you say, Keir, or how much you apologize, I'm about to make your life horrible.

I can barely open a can of soda.

And I also like soda.

A little bit.

Chapter 13

Mirelle.

So it's been like three days since we got Keir back.

But during these three days, he's gone really quiet. He gazes at the wall and he grows still and doesn't snap out of it until I tell him to. But I understand. Baron has tormented the living thing out of him physically, and mentally. Let alone what he's been through when he was young. So I'm staying here for a while. With my own free will. I visit mom and dad of course, but it's just me getting clothes, and eating.

Mom still was weird, all she asks about was if I was ok or not. And Jenny. And the others.

Dad still thinks Keir is Kevin.

And here I am. Staring at a zoned-out Keir, Finding the trees behind me interesting. His scarred eyebrow always twitches when he does that.

I mean if he was looking at me it would have been tolerated. Even I would admire myself.

"Are you just going to leave him like that?" Dylan whispered from beside me. "He looks like he saw an ants-filled bag of Doritos."

"Is that really your biggest nightmare?" I frown at him.

He walks back inside the house and mumbles something about him wanting Doritos now and that it is my fault.

I sigh and approach Keir carefully. "Keir," I call softly, but he doesn't look like he listened. "Keir," I repeat with the same tone. Now standing right in front of the wooden chair he's sitting on.

His blue eyes snap to mine.

Blue that carries millions of wonders under its waves.Blue that carries millions of miracles under its clouds.Blue that carries the depth of your eyes.

I memorize one page of his notebook.

"Sorry," he mumbles.

"Where were you?" I asked tilting my head.

He shakes his head rapidly. "Nowhere. Just thinking."

"About?"

"Just...nothing."

Again, not wanting to tell anyone.

Does he think we're stupid? I mean we might be, but not enough to not notice that he's suffering. Maybe I should leave him. I wouldn't want to be nosy, so I rise from my kneeling possible and get back inside the house.

"Wait," he ordered. I didn't take another step.

He stood from the chair and came to stand in front of me. "I- I wanted to apologize." His voice came out steady.

"You already did." I deadpanned.

"It isn't enough." He continued. "Look, I know you're mad and I deserve it, but I- when I saw you there and saw the missing money

I got mad and I did all of that, even though I knew you wouldn't do such a thing, I saw it. But I still defied it. And I'm sorry."

His hair is so gorgeous.

What?

Focus. I'm mad right now. "What if I was afraid of enclosed places? What if I had a heart attack and died?" I'm not the only one suffering from Dylan's undeniable optimism.

"You wouldn't-" his words faded.

I mentally snorted. "Or what if I was afraid of spiders and I saw a spider and there was no one to help me? What would you have done, Keir? Oh wait I know, it could be one of her tricks to get out of the room." I tried my best to mimic his voice.

I stare at him frustrated and all and wait for him to speak.

That's what I thought.

Is he aware of how fun it feels to scare him?

Yet I couldn't stop my thoughts from coming out of my mouth. "But, if you told me what were you thinking back there, I might forgive you. Just a little bit though."

He takes a long breath in, "I- fine."

"Please follow me on the chair, sir." I motioned him to sit back in the chair. Therapist mode activated.

He obeyed. Of course, he did. I know it's unbelievable but I could order him to go get Doritos for me and Dylan and he'll do it without thinking.

"Now, what exactly did you see?"

He sighed, "why do you want to know-"

"Answer the question."

He stared at me for a long time then cursed himself and leaned his back on the chair.

"It's my uncle, I keep thinking about him and what he says," he mumbled.

"What did he say?"

"That it is my fault. And that I deserve it." He eyed the ground.

Great, now I feel bad for him.

"Sir- I mean Keir." I start and he looks at me. "Do you really think it's your fault?"

He nodded.

"Why? What exactly did you do to make you think it was your fault?"

"I don't know, being born I guess."

"Keir don't be stupid more than you already are! Being born wasn't your choice and it wasn't your fault that your father left, you would've done nothing. He left because he wanted to leave, without having the intention to stay if just for you."

He doesn't blink, just stares at me with a serious look.

That is what I call the hawk face.

"Why?" he asked and I knew it wasn't about this topic.

Why does he care that much? why does he want to know that so bad? it's because I just...I had to do it.

"I don't like seeing anyone hurt, seeing you hurt," my mouth says against every thought that I wanted to say instead.

He looked...scared. But it didn't last long as he simply nodded. "Thank you, for everything. Not just for now, but for that day too."

I nodded. Not wanting to speak nonsense again.

He sighed and ran his hand through his hair. "You should've gotten inside. if you were hurt-"

"I know I know you wouldn't bear it and all." I pause. "Like I'd allow them to lay a hand on me! Did you even see how I tackled the man? For real, I was epic."

He still looked at me with that hawk face but then he chuckled.

Well, that was a sound I haven't heard in a while.

"Laugh all you want, I'll be giving courses on how to attack people and you'll just sit and watch."

When he's done laughing he says, "not to burst your bubble or anything, Mirelle, but you were going to get yourself killed."

I rolled my eyes at him and my eyes didn't meet his until I felt water drops landing on my face.

It started to rain.

I smiled at myself for that, I always loved the rain, I loved to make up stories of people dancing in the rain while I sat behind the window watching it.

I turned to Keir, finding him smiling at me too. "How do you feel? When the water touches you."

"It feels nice," he mumbled.

I smiled. "It doesn't seem like a threat, does it? Just playful and friendly, right?"

He nodded.

"Do you like it?"

"I do."

I smiled at that.

I wanted to dance, we were in the middle of the forest, there was water everywhere and I could jump in the small tiny puddles.

"Dylan!" He's silly and will agree.

"What?" He came running out of the house.

"Come dance with me," I tell him, and he doesn't waste time.

We sang and ran in the rain, and even jumped in the small water puddles. I loved that, it was as if we were characters in a book no one knew of, a scenario of little wild dances in the middle of the woods as it rains, and none but few knew of it. Yeah, that was lovely. Petrichor: pleasant earthly smell after rain.

Keir remained where he was, but he extended his arm to the rain, trying his best not to draw attention. It isn't as if I wasn't watching him for as long as he's alive. But he seemed happy. So it was okay.

But then Al came out of the house, covering her head with- I don't even know what that was. She said if we didn't all come inside in thirty seconds she'll come to pull our eyelashes.

With a glare.

Bless her heart.

So we all got inside. though all of us looked from the window, with the hot chocolate Al made us.

From the look on Keir's face, I knew he'd write about rain. And I'd read it. All of it. But what if I wrote for him this time?

I moved beside him. "Give me your hand."

He hesitated but extended his arm to me. I wait for a while, not sure if I should do this.

I approach my index finger to his hand, slowly. He doesn't take his eye off and his breathing becomes heavy. "Close your eyes," I order.

He drew his eye from my finger and our eyes connected. After all, a touch is nothing more than a look given by soothing eyes. He snaps his eyes shut.

"It's rain, it's just water, think of it this way."

His hands draw back a little bit. "Rain," I assure him, and he reaches for my finger again.

"It's okay," I tell him and he lets out a breath as an answer.

I hold his hand, slightly. Nothing more than a brush, like a touch of nature, like grass twirling under your bare feet.

He opened his eyes in surprise, not a flinch. He darts them to our collided hands, and then to my face. I could feel a smile forming on my face.

His eyes widen but he smiled back, widely. I could hear the sigh he let out.

I look at where Al and Dylan we're standing and I find them laughing. "If you told me you touched Keir's hand without him putting a knife through your chest I would have thought that you've got issues," Dylan blurts.

Well, guess what.

I turn my head to Keir again. "Feels like rain?" I ask him softly.

"Better," he whispers.

I drew my hands back slowly but Keir said. "Keep it." I looked at his face. He didn't worry looking at me as he admired our hands, he was happy. Mission accomplished.

I nodded, just because he has nice hair.

So we watched the rain, all of us. And he never took his hand away. And neither did I. He didn't zone out though. He just watches with a smile tucked on his lips.

It was only when the rain stopped that he let go of my hands and said, "thank you, I didn't think, that could ever happen." His eyes were full of gratitude.

I nodded in response, not trying to hide the happiness I felt.

And he walked inside to change his clothes.

I feel a hand on my shoulder and turn around to see Al's face. Awe glowed in her eyes. "Thank you," she said with a smile. "Again."

"Did you just smile?" I asked.

She deadpanned and walked away.

I'm sure she did. She didn't glare at someone for a while though-

"I told you to get out of the kitchen, Dylan!"

Oh, there she is.

Keir comes out with a clean white shirt and grey sweatpants looking happy. I mentally pat myself on the back for that.

Little by little. Step by step.

Better than rain.

Chapter 14

Mirelle.

I'm exploring.

I woke up today and I wanted to explore the woods. I have no idea where did that come from, but I'm doing it.

I've learned my lesson though, last time I walked through the forest at a late time Alana came from behind me and put a knife down my back. that's why I have a knife from the kitchen with me, and also because I want to be cool. I have no idea how to kill something, but I should manage, I've killed ants before.

Plus, I'm a strong independent woman. I am fear itself.

Now I don't know exactly where I am. But I do know that I'm far away from the house. And somehow I still manage to keep walking.

Confidence is the key. Even if you have no idea what you're doing.

I didn't see anything but birds and insects. I saw a little frog too. Thank God, none of them attacked me.

I heard something.

The wood on the ground was cracking as the sound neared me.

Maybe it's just a doe. Or maybe it's a freaking lion and will eat me on the spot.

Wait, I'll die by a lion eating me?

It approaches carefully. I should've told Dylan where exactly I was going.

Then it comes to view.

It's a bear. It's a freaking bear.

Its fur was brown, matching its eyes, I wouldn't know if I should look it in the eyes, but from the glimpses I took of its face, it carried no emotions on it. And so I figured it was a good thing. Or at least I only wished. It doesn't move. And neither do I.

What am I supposed to do? Oh, wait I know. Pray.

"So," I tell it. "It was nice to see you." I take a step to the back without looking, "I hope it never happens again though. Have a nice day, fella!" I take a few steps back quietly. It still doesn't move. And I took another step back.

I was falling.

It was down, so down. I realized it then. I was falling in a pit in the middle of the woods and it was deeper than Keir's poems. The bear didn't eat me. so I'll die in a pit.

Great.

I stopped falling.

I felt a slight pain in my head before it all went black.

Keir.

She wasn't here when I woke up, and I find myself already stressing out because she was supposed to be here. She came here more often now. I didn't notice I became used to her presence that waking up and not finding her sets me uneasy.

I couldn't help it anymore. "Dylan!" I called. "Where is she? Where is Mirelle?"

"Oh, I-" Dylan stuttered. "Listen, she told me she was going to explore. So I let her, I mean what am I supposed to say? No, you're not allowed to do as you wish-"

"Where is she?" I repeated carefully.

"She said she'll be back in an hour."

It's noon.

"Where is she?" I snapped.

"Around the area, I don't know," Dylan winced.

I'll stab him.

"And you didn't think it was important to tell me?" I paced around.

Dylan raised his arms."Keir, calm down." He wants me to calm down. And she's probably dead already.

"And you didn't even think about checking on her yourself!"

"What's wrong?" Alana said, running from the door frame.

"Dylan let Mirelle wander alone in the woods and it's been two hours."

She glared at Dylan. "Are you stupid?"

"We'll split up. Alana check at Jenny's and Dylan you go check her house. I'll go search in the woods." They nodded and moved in an instant.

"Dylan!" I called, And he turned his head to me. "If I didn't find her I'll kill you," I warned.

He swallowed and gave me a thumbs up then kept on his way.

He's going to make me lose my mind more than it's already lost.

I try to trace any kind of footprints on the ground or any broken twigs. I tried calling her name over and over. Nothing. I kept walking, focusing on the ground. And my dagger in my hand. Where could she be? This is a huge area. How on earth am I supposed to find her?

God.

I found something shiny, I ran to it as fast as I could.

A knife. Our knife. Then where-

I feel my heart pounding fast and I feel like my bones will come out of my hands and their trembling mess. She didn't move.

"Mirelle! Mirelle, are you okay?" I yell from over the pit she's in.

Immediately, I grabbed some tree branches and a stone and took off my jacket to wrap it around them. Then dropped them inside the pit. I got down carefully, not wanting to crack my skull too.

Please be okay.

I kneeled beside her and sucked in my breath, "Mirelle?"

"Mir," I said softly, shaking her.

"Wake up." I could feel the sweat on my face. "Please."

She didn't move.

"C'mon Mirelle." I took her hand in mine to check fur pulse. Alive.

"It's okay," I assure myself. "Man up."

I shake her harder, "Mirelle."

No. This can't happen.

"Mirelle, get up. Please," I whisper and I feel my throat tightening.

She moves her legs and then opens her eyes.

Thank God.

"Please don't eat me," she mumbles.

"What?"

She sits on her knees.

"A-Are you okay?" I asked hastily.

"Keir," she breathes. "Keir, you're here!"

"I thought I'd die here. You won't believe it. There was a bear and I fell here and I had a knife, where's my knife?" She twists around and searches for it.

"Shh," I said with a sigh of relief, "I have it. I have your knife."

What knife?

"Does your head hurts?" I ask.

"Yes." She brushed a hand over it. "But I'm fine."

"Can you stay like this?"

She nodded. "Yeah."

I took the small tree branches I got and using the stone, hammered them against the wall of the pit in levels; so it could be like stairs. There were six branches hammered in different levels until they reached the top of the pit.

I took a deep breath and turned to her, finding her clutching to her knife for dear life.

"Can you climb on my back?" I asked her.

"But you-"

"Just do it. Can you?"

She hesitated but nodded. So I walked up to her and waited until she climbed.

Rain.

I walked to the steps I built and stepped on the first tree branch. I kept getting upwards till we were both out of the pit. She then unwrapped herself from me as soon as we did so. And I allowed myself to scan her from head to toe.

She's fine, just a few scratches.

"Can you walk?" I asked softly, sweating too much, shaking too much.

She attempted to stand up but was going to drop right on her face. So I offered her my arm to lean on.

"Keir," she objected.

"I'm fine," I told her, "it's okay." It was not. But I'll do it.

So she did. With the freaking knife in her hand.

I just want to know what was she planning to do with it.

My breaths turn quick, and it turns out I'm breathing from my mouth the whole time. My hands were cold and pale.

But it's her. I kept reminding myself. It's just her. That alone put my mind at ease. A bit.

She leaned her head on my shoulder, her soft hair tickling my face. I gasped.

She drew back a little. "It's okay, it's just like the wind," she muttered.

I nodded because I didn't have it in me to speak.

I could feel her exhaustion so I tried to hurry to the house as fast as I can.

She's okay. She's by my side, safe and sound. I'm losing my mind.

Ten minutes later, I was half dragging her, half-dragging myself. I was in the same state though, but at least I could speak.

"Mirelle?" I ask her to clear my mind.

"Hmm."

"May I ask a question?"

"Sure."

"What in the worls were you doing out there?" I asked as friendly as possible.

"Exploring," she said it like it's the most obvious thing in the world.

"Great." I feel my left eye twitch and I guess that's a sign of a heart attack.

I can barely bear with Dylan for all I know.

"A request, maybe?"

She nodded.

"Please don't go anywhere outside without having one of us with you, especially in the woods. And don't ever listen to anything Dylan says."

She gave me a bored look. "What's your last name?"

"What?"

"What's your last name?"

"Striker."

She sighed. "Keir Striker, you are in no place to tell me what and what not to do."

I think I'm feeling my right eye twitch too.

"I'm sorry, love," I say as I walk half-carrying her.

We arrive at the house, Dylan, and Al was already there.

Dylan ran to Mirelle and threw her arms around her, "Mirelle," he said. "I thought I killed you. You have no idea how much Al kept yelling at me."

"I'm fine, I think I just need some rest." She laughed as she patted his back with her free hand.

Dylan took her arm and led her to the room.

I'm still going to stab him.

"Where was she?" Alana commanded. Alana's scarcely worried about anyone like that. She doesn't even like anyone for that matter.

"She fell in a pit, probably some hunter dug it for the bears or something."

She nodded, and looked back at where they got in, then turned to me. "She has her effect on you, you know." She smirked when she found me looking in the same direction. "Would you do the same if it was Dylan? you'd probably leave him to the bears."

He would scare the living thing out of them.

"And is that a bad thing?" I asked.

"No. It's not bad at all. I'm just happy for you."

I smiled at her. "I'm glad you like her too."

"Well, she keeps Dylan busy enough to stop talking."

I missed the happy Al.

"Let's go see her." I laughed, guiding her inside the house.

Dylan stood in a strange position trying to adjust the bandage on Mirelle's head. So with a glare from Alana, Dylan stepped away and let Alana deal with it.

Then we all sat on the chairs in the room. Mirelle told us about her trip in the woods and the bear. And that she took the kitchen knife to look scary. Alana glared at her this time, saying that she shouldn't go alone like that. And that she'll die if she listened to Dylan again.

Then she glared at Dylan again. Which in return gave her a devastating grin.

They just can't skip a day.

At least both of them were like a mother hen to Mirelle, telling her to not move every time she tries to.

After a huge argument with her and them convincing her to stay the night. They left at last. Leaving me alone with her.

I took the seat closest to her bed.

I did that a lot. It was always me protecting myself from everyone. Fearing the consequences of a simple touch, because I know them well. But when it came to her...I always wondered if there was no consequence in the first place. Or at least...maybe it's not that bad.

It felt nice. Not dangerous. It didn't hurt like I remember.

We stayed like that for a time before she said, "I love your writing."

I turned to look at her, frowning, "what?"

She let out a soft laugh, "I figured I'd have to tell you. The notebook in that drawer, I read it. All of it."

She took out my notebook from under her pillow showing it to me.

"You- you read it?" I've been searching for this for a while now, I figured it was lost somewhere so I got another one.

She nodded cheerfully, "I even memorize some of them, so you can say I'm your biggest fan."

"You know you could've just asked right?"

She looked at me like I'm stupid, "You locked me here, Keir. Do you expect me to just stay still and do nothing?"

Who am I kidding?

"Here, take this and write something. I want to see." She handed me the notebook with a pen.

What choice do I have but to listen to her?

I sighed. "Fine."

I opened the last pages of the notebook and prepared to start writing.

"When did you start writing?" she asked leaning her back on the bed headboard.

I looked at her. "Years ago, my mom bought me a notebook. This one. I wasn't really fond of the idea of telling someone how I feel, so I wrote it all down."

Her eyes softened. "I'm sorry I read it without telling you. But then again what was I supposed to do?"

"It's fine."

Her eyes are beautiful. Her hair is even prettier, she looks like the sunset. Free and full of energy. Her touch feels like it too, like the sun is passing its warmth for you, to have a little of the hope and life it possesses.

I turned my head to my notebook and wrote.

I'm falling. Too deep, there is no hope of getting out.It's almost pitiful, how low I've come to.It's you who's pulling me in, yet you have no idea what you're doing.The deeper I go, the warmer it becomes. It's like home, like I should've been there long ago.Falling is delightful.

She frowned at my faint smile. "Keir, it's beautiful and everything but I don't understand."

"I know."

Chapter 15

Mirelle.

"I want you to draw me like an avatar" I say dramatically and put a hand on my forehead.

Keir looks at me over his notebook with a soft smile of his. While Dylan throws his head back in laughter.

Keir doesn't want me to see what he's writing. And that's fine, I understand. Really. I mean it's not like I want to snatch it from his hands and read it just to mock him.

He suddenly closes his notebook shut and looks at us with a serious face.

Oh, boy.

"If you're going to say anything now, don't. I'm happy," Dylan said.

Keir sighed, "I assume I gave you the break that you needed. Procrastinating will do us no good." He looked at each one of us in the eye. "So I want you all to sit down here because I need to make some things clear."

I was the first one who sat down, of course. I would never miss an opportunity to feel like rich important people in a meeting.

After everyone settled in, Keir spoke again, "first of all, I want to thank you for all that you did for me that day. I appreciate every single thing you did to free me from Baron, specifically you, Mirelle."

I nodded like I knew what I was doing.

"For that, I still worked, but alone. I woke up early every day to hunt, and then I took it to the merchants myself."

"Wait, you worked without us?" Dylan asked, squinting his eyes.

"Yes. I did, and it was the least I could do. Anyways, thankfully, we have enough money to give Baron next month, that is if he showed up of course. Which I doubt he will."

"Why?" Alana asked.

"I think Baron is planning something way bigger than just that, I mean why do you think he didn't react about what happened. Is it Baron's like to be that calm?

"It's so obvious he's planning something." He darted his eyes towards me. "That's why we need someone to spy for us there."

Jenny.

But that's what he doesn't know. "I already knew you'd say this. I figured Baron would be trying to do something, so Jenny and I agreed that she should keep an eye on Baron every now and then, and get even closer to the guards."

His lips curled, "Excellent."

My heart flutters a little.

"We still have to be prepared though. From now on we'll practice every day. Keep your daggers with you," he said to Al and Dylan.

"Oh and Mirelle, please don't go stabbing criminals in the hand again," he said with a smile. "You're lucky he didn't kill you."

I would normally tell him that he's not allowed to tell me what to do. But I've learned my lesson. That's why I nodded quietly. And he flashed me a smirk for just that.

Dylan and Al got inside the house, talking about the orange juice Al will make.

"Uh, Keir?" I asked.

"Hmm."

I hesitated, "Do you want to go out for a walk with me?" He hasn't gone outside for a while, so I figured it would be nice to take him out.

"Like now?" he asked.

I nodded.

"Well, I guess- yeah sure I'd love that," he said but I still can see the worry on his face. Funny how he can be a leader with plans and all in a minute and then the other, he's like that. Worried? Afraid? Shy?

"Don't worry, there won't be a lot of people," I assured him.

He rose from his chair and walked inside the house to tell the others we're going out. When he came back, he had two jackets. He wore one and offered me the other. I didn't have a jacket, and it was cold. So I took it and put it on. It smelled just like him. trees, books, and rain. It was a little too big but it was fine. I still look perfect.

I offered him my hand, which he looked at hesitantly but he took it, slowly. We walked together, out of the woods.

"Are you for real? A children's playground?" he laughed.

Shame on him. He doesn't know how superior these are.

"Before you judge, Keir striker. Let me explain. first of all, see that truck over there? They have the best ice cream ever. That, and children are not brats here, well most of them aren't."

"Stop using my last name," he deadpanned.

"No."

He sighed and I led him to a bench so we sit together. I went to grab an ice cream, already knowing Keir's favorite, vanilla. And me, strawberry.

He didn't say anything about the ice cream though, but it was so obvious on his face that he loved it. It was sunset. and the sun was still here, so even though it was cold it melted our icecreams.

"Keir," I said. "Where did you get the scar on your eyebrow?"

He seemed...shocked by the question, a bit amused even. "You see, I was an energetic child. Once, Dad brought me to a playground like that, but I fell on my face and almost lost my eye. And it's there ever since."

I laughed, "I can imagine you just standing there and falling on your face. But it's beautiful it makes you even more...Keir."

He smiled. And that was one of the many things you won't see happen often.

"But I really want to ask you an important question though."

"Go ahead," leaning his back to the bench and lifting his head, letting the sun's warmth kiss his face.

"What's your hair routine-"

"Hello?" a little voice distracted me.

I look down at it to find a little girl with sun-kissed skin and black braided hair.

"Hi," I said, waving my hand at her. But she didn't seem to care, she just looked at Keir.

She's that young and still chooses the looks. I don't know what's wrong with little girls these days.

"Can you push me?" she asked innocently. Pointing her head to the swing behind her.

"I- me?" he stuttered.

Both of them are equally stupid.

"Uh- sure." He gave her a soft smile.

The girl ran back to the playground and sat on the swing waiting for Keir. And Keir standing up, my hand in his, walked to her pulling me behind him. He just doesn't get that I have opinions. I mean what if I didn't want to go? I did. but still.

Sweating, he put his hands on the girl's back and pushed her once. I squeezed his hand.

He pushed her again. "What's your name?" I asked.

"Kayla," she answered like I'm on her freaking nerves.

"Nice to meet you, Kayla. I'm Mirelle and this is Keir." She nodded like she didn't care.

I am not even kidding-

"We're leaving Kayla, let's go!" a tall woman called from a long distance, I didn't see her.

The girl got off the swing in a second. "Come back again, Keir." She smiled at him. "You'd always find me there with mommy."

And the weak idiot smiled back at her. "I will."

She threw me a warning look before she ran to her mother. As if nothing had happened.

I blinked. "On a scale of one to two, how scary would you rate this?"

"Like five," Keir answered honestly.

I sighed. "Easy for you to say."

He laughed, and we sat there back a little more time. And finally rose to leave with him clasping a hand on my back.

As we were walking back to the house, Keir cleared his throat, "I want you to meet my mom."

I shot my head back to him. "Really?" I whispered.

He nodded. "I go for a visit every now and then. I told her about you and she wants to meet you."

"Yes. Yes, I would love that, I wanted to see her too." Meeting Keir's mom. It's what I wanted since he first told me about her. Who knows what we can do. We can make fun of Keir for hours. She seems like the type who won't mind.

We walked through the empty streets, the faint shadows of the trees covering us as we walked, and the orange sun from the other side started to disappear. It was nearly nightfall now. Keir broke the silence, "Why were you scared of me?" His eyes darkened as they shifted back to seriousness.

"What?"

"That day, you know, you lied about getting lost because you were scared of me."

Where did that come from?

"It was just that you were a guy with a dagger and a cloak and I was a girl stalking you with a banana costume. How do you want me to react?" I answered sarcastically.

He looked hurt. "I'm still sorry, you know, I find it hard to trust people, anyone. But I trusted you, Mirelle, I liked you, but when I saw you there with the money gone, I believed the easiest thing I could think of." He looked at his feet, "I'm sorry I put you through all of this nonsense. I feel like a brute every time I think of it. I'm sorry I hurt you." His eyes darted to my face, hesitantly.

I took his hands. "You were stupid, obviously. But what's done is done. And I still happen to like you though, your hair-"

"You forgive me?" he interrupted, his eyes full of hope.

Why won't anyone let me know what he does with his hair?

But I sighed anyway, with a smile I said, "yes." I paused when the realization hit me. "You think of that a lot, don't you?" I asked.

I'm not saying that it isn't supposed to affect him. Maybe he should tell me what he feels even if it was just a part of it.

He nodded firmly.

"Keir," I say softly. "I know you think about your dad, your uncle, and Baron. But if you thought about your nightmares and your mistakes every second of your life what time do you really have to live? I know that letting go of these thoughts is hard, especially when you believe them. But be fair with yourself, look at you, look at your hands holding mine, you made a friend today, though she doesn't really like me. but you pushed her, willingly. And you looked happy doing it. Every time you think about them, take a breath and think about something else, talk yourself down and think about- think about me and my perfect face. You'll feel happy."

He laughed. Now I can think about that.

I can't stand watching him look that hunted, so to freshen up the mood I announce, "Three..."

"What?" he managed between laughter.

"Two..."

"You won't-" he tilts his head.

"One. Go!" I said and ran to the house, "you think you're the only one who can run? Well, take that, sucker!"

He laughed even louder and said, "you don't want to do that, Mir!"

Mir.

He started running to me. Three seconds and he was beside me, four seconds and he was already winning.

How the- this is not even physically possible, at least not for me.

It was eight at night when we got home, both of us panting and sweating. And laughing. We rested our hands on his knees while we panted. I don't know if we can even manage to speak at that point.

"You finally came," Dylan said behind us. when I turn to him, his face wasn't...Dylan's normal face.

Keir's smile faded from his face. "What's wrong?"

"It's him. He sent us a letter," Dylan said numbly. He handed Keir a paper. Keir took it and the color drained from his face as he read it, I moved beside him to read it.

You will regret this.Very much.

Chapter 16

Keir's nose flared. He handed the paper back to Dylan and strode to the house.

I followed him, calling his name over and over, but he didn't even turn to look at me. He got to his room and sat on his bed. When reached his room, I closed the door. I told myself that if he objected I'd leave immediately. He did not. I kneeled on my knees before him. He still didn't look at me, just stared at the floor, his hair falling on his face.

"Keir," I whispered. He didn't respond, he sat as still as stone, staring at nothing with his empty yet still hunted eyes.

I knew what was going on then.

"Keir, breathe," I told him, "look around you, look at me."

He slowly looked at me.

"Great. how do I look?" I ask him, swallowing.

"Sunset," he mumbled.

"What does my hair look like?" I asked him.

He didn't answer, but his eyes traced my hair as if the answer was only in his head.

"What's my eyes' color?"

"Hazel."

"What do you see around you?"

He stared at me, so deeply I didn't even know if he was there.

But then he covered his face with his hand and sighed. "I'm tired. I'm tired of this. Is it too much? To simply ask for a break?"

"No. No, it's not."

"I wish for this to be over, I wish to not think about what could happen if I lived as I want, I wish to-" he stopped and tightened his grip on my hand. He stood up, and so did I.

His face was still pale, sweating, even shaking a little. .

He turned colder, shook harder, and was panting. But still, he clung to me like I'm the last thing that can be touched.

He buried his face in my hair. "I'm scared," he whispered.

I nodded. "I know. it's okay. I'm here with you."

"Yeah."

We stayed like that, no one spoke, not awkwardly. Silence meant more than words did. I closed my eyes, for the best moments are not spoken, they're felt.

I spoke, "I'm proud of you."

That's it. that's what I wanted. if anyone is going to help him it's himself. I just thought I'd give him a little push to start, and for the first time, I succeeded.

He shook his head. "Me too."

Sometimes passed, he stood solidly. Nothing to be known about his face, sometimes he trembled really hard I would check if he was okay, the water on his face could be seen. And sometimes, he leaned in, and breathed rhythmically.

"Thank you," he whispered before finally, taking a step back.

He waited for me to say anything. But I just nodded and smiled.

And he hesitantly walked out of his room, calling Alana's name.

He did it. He survived and did it.

I stood there in his room, not quite believing what just happened. Before he turned back and told me he needed me outside. Well, not that but, "we need your Sherlock Holmes self outside." And who am I to reject such an offer?

They all gathered around a table. Everyone took a seat already only one seat was left empty, for me. I took it, feeling that finally a place was made just for me.

In the middle, was the Baron's letter. As Al said.

"As you all saw," he pointed to the letter. "Our beloved Baron sent us a reminder of what he'll do."

I like the way he thinks he's the protagonist when he talks in these little gatherings.

I also like his hair.

"Now, we don't know exactly what he's doing or how far he'll go, though we do know it's very far. Whatever he'll do we should be prepared for it. As I said, you both should start your practicing tomorrow. If they came here we stand, holding our ground and fighting. We have to protect what we hold dear to us, including ourselves even if it'll cost us the world." He darted his eyes to me and looked away again.

"And Dylan, stop being stupid," he said at last.

Dylan threw his pen on the table and stomped his hands on it. "What did I do now!"

Keir shrugged. "Nothing, in particular, you just seem stupid."

"The- what- Mirelle, tell him to stop I know you love me."

He did seem stupid though. But I love him.

"Stop it, Keir, even if he's stupid don't hurt his feelings like that," I said. Keir looked like he was holding back a laugh and Al smiled.

Dylan had a 'really?' Look all over his face.

"You didn't have orange juice," Al said, rising from the chair. "I saved you some after that wierdo tried to have it all to himself." She glared at Dylan.

"Why does everybody hates me today? It's not my fault you don't feed me."

She made an effort not to slap him, I saw it. and walked to the kitchen.

People can do hard things indeed.

"Bring the cookies with you!" Dylan called.

And Al took a knife from a drawer loud enough for us to hear.

"Fine. You could've just said it," Dylan said, shrinking into his seat.

Dylan is such an icon. He takes too many threats and he still lives like a cat. Only worries to be fed.

"Some people just don't appreciate me," he sighed.

I smiled at him just to assure him but apparently, that wasn't enough. "Keir, when we were saving you I saw a bug on the floor-"

Keir interrupted him, "Dylan, I don't care about any bug," he said, toying with Baron's letter.

Dylan just brushed him off and turned to me, "I'm not kidding, Mirelle, it was that big." He gestured to his palm.

"I'm pretty sure she doesn't care either but go on," Keir mumbled.

"Anyways, it was in the way and I didn't have a choice but to-"

Al came with a tray of orange juice on it, glaring at Dylan, she set it on the table.

Keir took his glass and when I tried to take mine Dylan was already laying his hand on it. But Al hit his hand, he drew back quickly, examining it for any injuries. Then she handed me mine.

"So what happened to the bug?" I asked, kind of curious. Alana sighed in disappointment and Keir did a facepalm.

"Oh, yeah the bug. So I thought it was really cute and all but I also thought of Al. She's scared of bugs."

"I'm not. They just gross me out."

"They gross her out. So I had no option but-"

"But to what?" I said trying to sound as serious as possible.

"But to-"

"What did you do?" I slowly stood up from my seat.

"Killed it," he whispered, numbly.

"You murderer!" I yell, pointing a finger at him as Keir does. And he noticed and shakes his head with a smile on his face.

"I had no other choice!" Dylan shakes his head in denial. "What else would I have done?"

"Well, wasn't that just tragic," Keir said.

"Just sit down and drink the st-" Al warned.

"The juice. Drink the juice, Mirelle." Keir shot her a glance. I laughed but did sit down to drink my juice.

When I'm done I tell Al that it was wonderful and stand up to leave. "I should get going, it's getting late."

It was always hard when I left, I wanted to stay with them and mess with them, but mom said it, we had a house.

It was when I was halfway through the trees that I felt a hand on my wrist. I felt my heart drop to my feet as I turned to see who it was.

"Calm down, it's just me," Keir said putting his hand before his face in defense.

I let out a sigh. "What is it? Is something wrong?" I said, scanning his face.

"No, it's just-"

"What's wrong, Keir?"

He stayed quiet for some time then he took in a breath.

"Stay," he said searching my eyes for an answer.

"I can't, my parents will be worried if I didn't go home."

He shook his head. "Not just today."

I blinked at him. "Like forever?"

"Forever."

Stay. What a strange request, it even sounded unfamiliar in my ears. No one ever asked that. It was either being left or being told to leave.

Why? Why me? What did I do to deserve to stay?

"Why?" I breathed.

"We need you. I need you." He didn't hesitate to answer.

"You've already become one of us," Dylan said walking from behind a tree, panting as if they ran all the way to here. Al was in the same state.

"It's been a while since we met," Al said. "Never have I ever felt like I had a true friend who acted like a....sister."

This was just too much. I couldn't take it.

Did I get too used to rejection that even just appreciation is foreign to me?

"It- I can't," I said feeling my throat tightening.

"Why not? You're old enough to move out," Keir suggested.

"It's not that." My voice got raspy.

"Do you not want to?" Keir asked softly.

"No! I would love that."

"Then what is it?" Alana asked.

Don't cry. Don't cry. Don't cry-

I burst into tears. "It's because what's the point of that? Why would you want from me? I'm just a fool in the way. What good do I do except talk a lot?" I wipe away the tears though there's more getting out. "You already have enough problems to deal with. I won't be one of them. I'm selfish and arrogant and useless and- why don't you see what the others see?" Looking at each one of them, I saw concern in their eyes.

Only Keir, that I saw was shock and hurt and...rage.

He took a step towards me, "Oh, Mirelle." His face softened then. "Have you forgotten what you said? Or what you did? Be fair with yourself, Mir," Keir muttered. He took a step to the front and another and continued till we were only inches apart.

I could have sworn I heard a gasp behind me.

For a moment everything and everyone was quiet. Even the trees didn't move. And the wind suddenly stopped, as if nature itself didn't believe this was possible. He stayed in his position, his heart never getting rest.

My tears eventually stopped falling.

He pulled away, face white as snow but smiling.

"Stay with us, be one of us. You're not a discomfort. You're useful to us in every way possible, not just Baron. You're our friend. And you're perfect. And whoever says otherwise is most definitely blind," he said.

Dylan patted my back and Al still looked concerned.

"I'm okay. I'm okay," I assure them.

"No one mentioned that before, but there's literally no one else who cared about my bug story." Dylan smiled.

"Maybe because you said it like a hundred times." Al glared.

I chuckled and they all looked pleased with themselves. "I wouldn't want anyone not to care about your bug, Dylan."

"See? That's what a true friend is!" Dylan said to Both of them.

I wipe my face with my sleeves. "It will just take time to move, you know and it's already risky to move a lot with Baron around."

He smiled. "That's why I brought both of them. To help you."

I laughed but it was more like a sigh. Dylan took my hand and we strode to my house.

We all stood outside my parents' house, waiting for them to open the door.

My mom opened it, the surprise on her face wouldn't have been more obvious. She looked at Keir. "You're fine."

She smiled when she saw his confusion. And opened the door wider for us to get in.

Dad was watching TV when he turned to see us, he arches his brow. "Well, hey Kevin."

Mom shot him a glare, dad turned back to his TV.

Alana would be proud.

"I'm sorry, Keir." She gave him a motherly smile.

He sat on a chair before her. "It's fine," he said.

"Since you're all here I would like to clear some stuff up." She sat and motioned for us to do the same. "See, I...was already going to make this conversation some way or another. But I just didn't find the right time."

She's been like that since the day they visited me at Keir's house. She'd normally sit with me when we eat and laugh at dad, but ever since what happened, she's been...off.

"Mom, what's wrong?" I asked.

She paused and her eyes reddened as they became full of tears, "I was so worried about you," she shook her head. "Jenny told me about everything since she was working with that Baron. I wanted to take you back by any means even if they'd take me instead. But she said that you should stay and that she needed you with them, that they'll protect you."

Dad stilled.

She knew? All along?

That's why she was off that day. Worry must've eaten her alive. and I didn't even know or notice anything all these days.

I didn't realize I was crying until a tear slipped from my face.

I look at Keir to see his reaction, only to find the hawk face.

"So I wanted to thank you, for everything you did, and for keeping her safe," she said to all of them.

Keir swallowed, I don't know if it was the words he was going to say or the words my mother said that made him nervous but there, "I want her to come live with us." His words spilled like wine.

Dad turned to us. "Excuse me?"

"Dad, I'm eighteen. I can move," I tell him as respectfully as I can manage.

"No!" He flared and stood up. "You've gotten yourself in enough trouble already, you're not going anywhere."

If he only knew that was only the beginning.

"Thomas," my mom warned with warning eyes, though there was sadness buried in them. "The boy's proven himself."

He approached us, "Nancy, she's my daughter," he said weakly.

I've never, never seen him that desperate. I never knew I could want something more than to comfort him. But...Isn't that life?

"She's my daughter too," she said with the same tone.

She turned to me. "Are you okay with this? do you really want to go?"

I nodded.

"Then go." She waited. "But please, visit. every day if possible."

I hopped off the couch to her and hugged them both as tightly as I could. "Thank you. I'll miss you." My voice came out wet with tears.

They both held me. "We'll miss you too, Mir. We'll miss you too."

I let go and went upstairs to pack. I pack my clothes, my blankets, and my books, of course.

When I was done. My parents were telling them that I'd die if they didn't give me breakfast. And possibly all my life stories.

I clear my throat, "I'm ready." And they all move to my side to help me with the bags.

"Keir," my dad called. "Keep her safe." His voice darkened.

Keir held my dad's eyes but nodded and said, "I promise."

I said my goodbyes and I cried as we did. I'm sure it's fun living with Keir and the others, but I can't help but remember the eighteen years I've spent with my parents. Or every time I woke up having a nightmare running to my mother's warm hug. Or the days I used to help dad fix broken stuff in the house. Or our movie nights.

It's okay. I tell myself. I'll visit and call every day.

When we got home it was already midnight. So all I did was go to bed.

Chapter 17

Mirelle.

I didn't wake up in my bed today, not in my room. I didn't hear my parents arguing. And that breaks my heart a little. Because for once, I yearn them yelling about who ate the other's food.

But I remind myself that I have my friends here, and I can visit my parents whenever I wish. And that my parents are probably fighting over how they ran out of milk now. So, carefully, I drag myself out of bed and stride to the bathroom to take a quick shower.

When I was done, I searched for them inside the house and I didn't find them, I searched for them outside, they weren't there either. The house was washed with silence.

I begin to worry as I call their names over and over. But it's like they've never been here.

They're kidnapped. There's no other explanation.

I was about to get outside again to search in the woods but I felt something behind me. I turned to see it, expecting to find nothing like in horror movies.

But instead, three people were standing with black cloaks and knives in their hands.

I didn't know what to do between running and screaming. So I chose the easier part and screamed.

It was a few seconds after, that I realized who these figures were. So I stop screaming and let out a sigh. "I hate you."

They all burst into laughter as they let their hoods down.

"I mean...why?" I laughed with them.

Both Dylan and Al ran toward me -and scared me again- but to my surprise, they hugged me tightly.

"Welcome, Mir," Dylan beamed.

"Thanks, Dylan," I say as I hug them back.

I glance a look at Keir, he was standing smiling, a true one. His eyes glitter with joy as he watches us. And I find myself smiling at that too.

They finally pull back and they all just looked too delightful.

"I'm glad you're here Mirelle," Keir says smiling and I feel my lips slide to a smile right away.

"Liar," Dylan said "he's not just glad, he's on cloud nine. My boy stayed up all night planning this." This time it was Keir who glared at him, but the pleasure in his eyes didn't fade away.

Dylan hooked his hand with mine and ran outside the house and played music, loud enough I can't hear Al screaming.

And that's epic.

Dylan holds my hand and twisted me around and pulled me back to him I twisted him and then we kept jumping around like fools.

Keir and Al came out of the house, though I couldn't miss the hand Keir laid on Al's shoulder.

Dylan let go of me and run to Al. She hisses at him of course but that never stopped him. He wrapped his hands around her waist and swayed to the rhythm of the music. Al glared at him, but in return, he gave her that charming smile of his.

I walk back to Keir who didn't move from his place. "Why aren't you dancing?" I ask him as I finally stand beside him.

He gives me a look that says 'don't act stupid.'

I look at Dylan and Al swaying with the music, and can't help but smile at how cute they looked.

"Dance with me," I tell him, or more like command him.

He scans my face and the daring look I give him. "But I-"

"No buts, you're doing great already. Now punch fear in the face and dance with me Keir Striker."

His eyes switch from me to Alana and Dylan, he looks at me again and takes in my face, and smiles a little before stretching out his hands.

As he should.

I take it carefully and he leads me to where Dylan and Al are dancing.

"Just for two minutes, I promise," I whisper to him and he only smiles knowingly and tucks a fallen hair behind my ear.

We twist and turn and sway and swing, all with music dancing with us, our feet crashing with the wet grass under it. Our limbs became one as they moved together in sync. Music became one with the dance. I leave myself to him at last, unable to catch up with his skill. We waltz again and he spins me like they do in castles.

He doesn't move for a while, and neither do I. We looked so deeply into each other eyes, and I wished he knew what he was looking for because I didn't. And I find myself lost in his blue eyes again.

Pull yourself together. I tell myself, yet I don't.

"Why didn't anyone tell me that you out of all people can dance?" Dylan marvels at Keir.

Keir pulls away from me and looks at Dylan. "Dylan."

"Yes?"

"Shut up."

Dylan nodded and continued doing what he was doing.

"The stupid thing Kept stepping on my foot the whole time and now I'll have to punch him," Al said monotonously.

I don't know how to mention it to them, but I really can't dance. It was all Keir. But I won't tell them so they think I'm cool too.

"Now that you had fun," Keir starts, "and that we all welcomed our dear Mirelle properly." He smiles at me. "Daggers out and fight," he commanded.

Dylan deadpanned and rolled his eyes, but in an instant, he and Al stood in front of each other.

Dylan jabbed for Al with his dagger. But Al dodged his wrist with her arm, though that didn't stop Dylan, as he continued to close the distance between Al and his dagged, and it touched her.

"Stop," Keir interrupted, "for the million times, Al. Don't only use your arm, use your whole body to dodge the attack. And you," he darted his eyes to Dylan. "Don't actually kill her, you idiot."

Al nodded, Dylan struck again and aimed for her shoulder but she twisted her hand around his wrist and pulled him, letting him nearly fall. She pointed her dagger at Dylan's back. "Loser," she mumbled to Dylan when he finally fell to the ground.

"Good," Keir said to Al. "Dylan, don't just try to win, be sure that your opponent can easily dodge you and kill you, hit where they least expect."

He nodded and they continued their sparing.

I decided I should get inside the house and eat something. But before I stepped inside I saw a piece of paper folded like the other one from Baron.

"Uh...Keir?" I called as I bent down to take the paper.

In a moment he was beside me, "what is it?" he said with a concerned tone.

I quietly handed him the paper and looked down at it.

"Everything okay?" Dylan asked from where they were fighting.

Keir nodded, "Continue."

We both got inside and sat at the table, Keir took the seat beside me. He unfolded the paper, read what it said, and gave it to me.

Eyes are everywhere.

He's got issues.

"What now?" Keir asked, desperately.

I had no answer, not really. So I just patted his back and tried my best to show understanding.

He frowned and leaned unto the wall, "I mean what am I supposed to do now?"

"Nothing, do nothing for now. It's okay," I answered him softly.

I heard loud footsteps approaching us, and then Al came into view.

"What is it? What did he say?" She frowned and her face was red, I don't know if it's because she moved a lot or because she was furious.

I gave her the paper, and she snatched it and read it.

"What does that mean?" she asked. Putting the paper on the table.

"I don't know. Just go practice," Keir said with a dull voice.

"Keir, I'm not leaving now-"

"I said go," he demanded. "What are you going to do? What are we going to do? We have no chance against him." He sounded defeated. And if I could rip Baron's throat out for even daring to break him, I would.

She waited, but eventually, she nodded and left.

He sighed and stood up. "Come, let's get outside," he said and walked to the door.

Dylan and Al we're still fighting. There was something off with them, but I didn't have to wonder what happened.

We sat in front of them, Keir commenting on some of their movements and them improving as I watch like I know what was going on.

"I really don't know what to do anymore," Keir said after telling Dylan to control his distance for the hundredth time. "Either I put your head in a blender or put mine and be done with it."

"Calm down, Keir. We need patience here." I tell him even though I know it's none of my business.

He shakes his head. "He's going to get himself killed," he mumbled.

He turns his head back to them and suddenly stands up, "Yes, Alana, knee him. He deserves it!" And Alana didn't even think about objecting.

Uh...Violent?

I went to check if Dylan was okay, but my arm hit a tree.

And when I looked up I saw something.

A person.

It hid back behind a tree quickly, but I already saw him. Maybe he's lost like I was.

"Who are you?" I ask.

No seriously, I need to stop being stupid. Why did I ask that? Like what are they supposed to say? Oh, don't worry I'm just here to kill you?

The laughter faded. And in a moment, they were all standing in front of me.

"What did you see?" Keir demanded with a low, wary voice.

"I don't know, it was someone." I pointed to the tree I saw the person at. "There."

A guy came out of the tree, holding his hands up in defense. He didn't look so much older than Keir. But Keir was taller.

"Please calm down, I just need help," he said carefully.

"Who are you?" Keir commanded. His voice came out louder than before.

The boy swallowed and approached us, Keir took a step back and extended his dagger at the boy.

Control your distance.

"Woah! Easy there, I'm Adam. Adam Danielson."

Keir eyes him. "What are you doing here?"

I tried to step from behind them to see the guy, but Keir pushed me behind him again softly.

What?

"I just- I was walking around. You know, people do that. And I kind of got lost, so I tried to track someone, anyone who might help me find my way back. And it was you." He said easily.

I pushed my way to the front again but Al glared at me.

I'm pretty sure the guy saw me already. And it's not like he'll eat me.

So I slid under Keir's arm he put to keep me behind him, and I took a good look at the guy.

He had sandy hair and hazel eyes. "Well, hello there," he greeted.

What does he think I am? Five?

"Hello," I greeted anyways. Trying my best to sound like the strong independent woman I am.

"Why were you hiding, beautiful?" he asked, grinning down at me.

I feel Keir stiffen beside me.

I open my mouth to tell him that it's none of his business but Keir speaks.

"Walk straight ahead, you'll find yourself out of here."

Adam still doesn't take his eyes off of me, he eyes every single part of my body from head to toe. I swallow and open my mouth but nothing comes out. Keir takes my wrist and carefully draws me behind him again, this time I don't say anything.

The guy still scanned me and took a step towards me, so I took a step back.

"Leave," Keir demands, his grip tightening around my wrist.

Adam noded. His eyes finding focus on Keir's face. "I'm sorry to disturb you," he said and left as Keir instructed him.

It's okay, Not everyone feels safe after all.

Chapter 18

Keir.

"Keir, please," Dylan says as he duels with Al. She strikes at his leg, he uses the Prasada method and dodges her attack with his dagger as a shield, then goes for a thrust near her neck. For once I'm thankful he does as I say. "I want to do anything."

They've been whining over this nonstop. Especially Dylan. I won't do it, I don't want to do it.

I put one leg over the other. "Your silence is enough to me."

He halted, "I'm not kidding, you always do everything on your own. It's time to let us help."

I eyed him. "You are going to get yourself hurt."

"And you won't?" he scoffed, "I mean it's not like you're the only one who can't get hurt."

"I'm-"

Al approached us. "I'd hate to say it, but he's right Keir. We understand you don't want anyone hurt, but you can't put it all upon yourself, it's our problem. Not just yours."

Dylan smiled wildly. "You didn't just-"

"Shut up," Al continued, "Keir, we don't want you in trouble as much as you don't want us."

"I'm more trained than you. I know techniques that you don't."

Al rolled her eyes. "And we know stuff you don't. we've been through stuff you didn't go through, we know people you don't. This isn't about you."

I wanted to say no. I did. But they won't stop. So I fought every piece of common sense left in me, and said, "Fine. Go see what Baron is planning."

"How?" he asked.

"However you see. But Dylan, if you got yourself in trouble, it'll be on you." I say, though I know I'd hate myself for it.

He blinked and took a step back. "I'll do it. And you'll see." He ran to the opposite side of the house.

I didn't look away from him until he faded from view.

I knew this was wrong. I knew I was supposed to protect them not send them to danger itself. But I promised them, I promised I'd involve them in everything. And that my problems are theirs too. But worry is eating me alive, and I can't do anything. I want to protect them all, but protecting someone is not that easy.

I look at Al, she still stared at where Dylan has gone. So to ease the tension I said, "Come, show me your moves, Al."

A soft smile drew itself on her face, drawing her dagger, we started.

Mirelle.

Standing in front of the milk shelf I question my whole life decisions.

I probably shouldn't have volunteered to buy the groceries. I mean I don't even know what I'm doing at this point. And it's my fault, buying milk is not that hard.

I know what to do.

I closed my eyes and randomly grabbed a bottle.

That's it. that's the one.

I put it in the cart. And look back at the milk. What if they want chocolate milk.

This just hurts my brain.

I'm thinking about calling my mom again. I'd do it. It's just that she threatened to block me after I called her for the hundredth time asking her what kind of cheese is the best.

I really don't know what kind of mother she is. She should be happy she hears my beautiful voice anyway.

Dylan told me to get him Doritos. So I got myself too...like five or something.

I got a new book!

I was about to check out when I felt someone touch my shoulder. Scared, I pull away and look behind me, ready to punch him in the gut.

My head smashed a hard chest. I think my head is spinning. If there was a chance this person wouldn't kidnap me, I just lost it.

I heard soft chuckles then. But when I look up to see who's that-

Oh.

It was the guy from yesterday. Who knows what his name was.

"Well, hello there..." he greeted with a smile.

"Mirelle," I deadpanned.

He frowned but still didn't stop smiling. "That's...a unique name"

I know.

"Thank you," I said instead.

He bent to grab my bags and walked out of the store.

"No, you don't have to." I objected as I went to grab the bags. That's pretty weird and uncomfortable if you ask me.

"It's okay, I want to walk you home."

"I-"

"I insist," he pressed.

I'll hit him with the bag in his head.

I sighed, "fine."

He smirked and we walked together, not giving him any attention I walk straight to the house.

"I wanted to apologize." He broke the silence.

I turned my head to him. "For what?"

He sighed, "when I showed up yesterday, you seemed...irritated."

We walked into the woods. "It's fine." I watched my feet as I spoke, normally I'm extroverted. But it's all about the people I guess.

"No, it's not. I'm really sorry, Mirelle." When I didn't answer he added, "and the other fella, he didn't seem so welcoming."

My head turns to him at the mention of Keir.

"Who is he anyway? Is he some kind of bodyguard?" he chuckled. "He seemed so protective of you. Are you that important to him?"

I could feel the heat rising to my face. So I turned away. "It's just his nature. He doesn't really like people, especially, in his territory." I explained as I recalled what he did when we first met. I almost snorted.

"We could be friends, you know," he said after a long pause.

What would Jenny say? She was always suspicious about boys asking to be my friend out of the blue.

I missed her, it's been a week or more since I last saw her. but I did call her every day, after I call my parents of course, though I'd rather see them face to face.

She would probably tell me to slap him and go get a pizza. Which is not a bad idea. So I fully turned to him to picture that happening.

He smirked. "What? Want a picture?"

I shook my head and continued walking.

If only he knew.

When we got to the house Al and Keir were combating. It's not even weird anymore.

No sign of Dylan.

As we approached them, they noticed I was there. And in return, Keir gave me a wide smile that reached his eyes. Until he noticed. ..whatever his name was.

"Adam," Keir mumbled. "What are you doing here?"

Oh yes. Adam.

"I met Mirelle at the grocery store. And I mean who would miss the opportunity to walk her home?"

In these times I wish I could summon Jenny here.

"She would've managed by herself just fine," Al affirmed.

Wow.

He rubbed his neck. "Well, I just wanted her to have company."

She stepped towards him, dagger in her hand. "She has just the right company," she said grimly.

Adam shifted on his feet. "I just-"

Al turned her head to one side. She stared at him like she could see his insides. If it were up to her she'd stab now and there. "But we appreciate it," she said, forcing the words out of her mouth, and stepped back beside Keir.

She's a baddie.

I give her a look of gratitude. And looked back at Keir's face.

The hawk face.

But he looked back at me and I understood what I had to do instantly. I walked to stand beside him.

"So daggers huh?" Adam finally asked.

Keir shrugged and dropped the dagger in his pocket.

"So you want to take me on a dagger combat?" Adam invited.

Keir halted and turned back to him after walked away. "You can fight?" he asked.

"I bet I can take you down," Adam challenged.

Well, I bet not Adam, just watch him controlling his distance.

Where's Dylan?

"I like a challenge," Keir accepted. "Alana, give him your blade."

She hesitated but obeyed. Though she gave Adam a look that said 'if I find a scratch on it I'll scratch your whole face.'

Adam just smiled and took it, and without hesitation, he struck at Keir.

Adam aimed for Keir's left shoulder, but Keir blocked his attack with his forearm. And aimed for Adam's foot.

But Adam was fast. He spun quickly, the hit had gone in vain. Keir managed a thrust again. But Adam whirled and prevented the attack.

Adam fought well. And from Keir's clenched jaw, He knew that too.

Adam attempted a slash at Keir's torso. But Keir kept moving in circles, moving his dagger so fast, it was hard to see it.

Adam drove forward harshly.

Keir's features turned to a pained frown as the dagger slashed through his bicep. But he didn't even try to look at it, he just continued fighting as though nothing has happened.

Keir lunged forward, doing a thrust, and disarming Adam in the process.

I wish I could cheer but the circumstances were not so handy. And besides, Al was beside me. I didn't dare make a move.

I thought it was over but Keir did not relent, Keir kept thrusting forward, not giving Adam a chance to do anything but to dodge some of Keir's attacks with his top arm and take a few steps back.

Keir managed a slash on Adam's wrist, not too severe.

But Adam fell on his stomach like a flash of light and grabbed Keir's foot. Sending him down on his back.

Keir shifted to his side aiming his dagger at his neck, and cut a layer of Adam's skin so slight, it was hardly there.

"I win," Keir whispered with a managed smile, before rising to his feet. Leaving Adam panting on the ground.

I turned to Al to check if she saw what I just saw. Only to be met with a one-sided smirk.

Keir is so cool, like what.

Eventually, Adam stood up too. His smile returning. "Impressive."

"I know right," I squeaked and kept jumping from one leg to another, beaming at how much of a great fighter he is.

Adam crossed his arms over his chest. And only smiled and shook his head. "I still don't know who you are," Adam said, approaching Keir.

Keir ignored him, picking Al's dagger from the ground and handing it back to her.

"Mirelle, tell me his name," Adam said, tilting his head to one side.

As Keir, I didn't answer too.

"As you like. I just wanted to know my opponent's name." Adam pressed.

Keir raised his eyebrows. "Is that so?" He eyed Adam, "Keir," he said, finally.

"Keir," Adam repeated. His eyes carried the satisfaction they craved for.

"And you?" he asked Alana.

She lifted her eyes to his, boringly, she said, "You're not worthy of knowing."

Adam smiled. "Right." He tooka step back, "I'd like to take you out, Mir. Is that okay with you?"

Al didn't look away from his face. But Keir, he looked at me, scanned my face. As if looking for the answer himself.

His arm was bleeding.

"I'm sorry Adam. I have to do some stuff. Maybe later," I said.

He shook his head, still smiling, he said, "It's fine. See you...tom orrow?"

I don't want to be rude, but I don't want to go either. I don't want to make anyone feel out of place or disliked.

So I sighed, "fine then, meet me here first."

His eyes glimmered with his smile. "Perfect," he said and finally left.

I turned back to Keir and Al.

"What is actually wrong with you!" Alana snapped at me.

"What?"

"You could have said no if you didn't want to go, Mirelle," Keir said, Crossing his arms over his chest.

But he'll feel bad.

"I know but-"

"There are no buts. You could've told him you didn't like him, and that you're staying here. With the people you love so much. If you're not comfortable just say no," he said, his face growing serious now.

Why is he so mad about this?

"Your arm is bleeding."

"Let it bleed!" he snapped.

Keir, I promise you don't want to be on my bad side.

I walked to him, gripped his other arm, and dragged him to the bathroom.

"Sit down," I ordered.

He hesitated. Still not even looking at me.

"You're going to bleed out and die," I added.

He sat down.

His bicep compared to mine was like comparing a cow to a frog. He could probably carry a cow. Cool.

that's it. I'm working out and I'll be a cool girl. And I'll also carry a cow.

"Do it," he urged, with the attitude.

The wound was full of blood. It looked disgusting, but it wasn't that bad though.

So I cleaned around it, as softly as I can manage.

"If you didn't stop being rude and not speaking to me I'll punch you in the face," I said as I continued cleaning his wound.

"I'm not being rude," he defended himself shortly after.

"Then talk to me or I'll punch you in the face."

"You can't"

"Watch me."

He bit back a smile, but I could see it clearly.

I took the bandage and wrapped it around his arm, trying my best not to hurt him.

"You're so dramatic," I say, "I mean all that because I'll go out with him?"

He opened his mouth to say something, but he closed it, paused a little and then said, "I don't like him."

"You don't like anyone," I rolled my eyes.

"Not true, I like Al and even Dylan and...you."

"You like me?" I asked, smiling a little. A lot.

He nodded.

"Aw, that's so sweet." I poked his cheek. "I like you too, Keir."

He rolled his eyes at me. But smiled.

When I was done I stepped away from him.

He extends his arm, checking if it works, and walked outside, he paused, waiting for me to follow.

"Where's Dylan?" I asked.

He froze, "I...sent him to see what Baron's up to." He looked at the floor as he walked.

I was worried about him, that was a little...too dangerous. But I guess that's what we had to do anyway. I'll pray that he comes home soon, safe and sound. So I didn't speak.

I followed Keir outside, I always do. I show him the book I got and I make him act all interested, even if he doesn't care I'll make him.

He bends down and plucks a flower, a yellow one that's shaded with orange. "It looks like you." He smiled to himself. "Keep it as a bookmark."

I took it from his hand and pressed it between my book. I watch him as he stretches his back on the chair and lets the sun rays tickle his skin.

I like you.

I trace the flower he gave me as I stare down at it. I don't know why it mattered so much. It just did.

Chapter 19

Mirelle.

"You should seriously consider getting a monkey," I said as I walked to Keir, sitting on a chair outside the house.

"Sure," he mumbled, not listening to me.

"I'm serious, I'm even naming it Keir."

The line of his lips stretched on his pale face in a smile, and I smiled back because that was my goal in the first place.

"You're naming what Keir?" Al asked, smirking a little as she walked towards us.

"I'm getting a monkey," I told her.

She blinked. "Oh."

I was going to speak again, but I heard something behind me that sounded like footsteps, it was coming closer. I stand still, feeling Keir and Al do the same.

I almost gasped when I saw who was there.

Standing before me was someone wearing a cloak, though when he took it off I felt my heart reach my feet.

Dylan. His face was full of blood, and he was struggling to stand without swaying.

"I'm like seventy-five percent sure I'm going to collapse right now." He tried to sound like everything's cool but obviously, it isn't.

I did not let temptation overtake me as I ran towards him. "Oh my Gosh, Dylan," I wrapped his arms around my neck and led him inside to his room.

"I still look handsome, don't I?" Exhaustion filled his voice though he kept on a light smile.

This was all wrong. We shouldn't have let him go, he's too dumb to survive.

I didn't answer him. But as we walked I glanced at Keir, his eyes widened a little, and his face was white. Al was not so different.

We enter the house, and I notice Dylan struggling to stand. I set him on his bed and rest his head on the pillow.

I heard Keir's angry footsteps approaching us.

Oh boy.

"What did you do?" Keir interrogated, rage flaring in his eyes. Al came after Keir.

"The one thing you asked me not to do," Dylan answered simply.

"What happened, Dylan!" he snapped.

Dylan attempted to sit up, but I pulled him down again, trying to clean the blood from his face. I shook my head at him to tell him to stay like that.

"Keir, I promise I watched my distance," Dylan tried.

"You didn't!" Keir pointed his finger at him.

I finished Dylan's face and stepped away. It looked better, but the bruises are definitely there.

"I need you to relax, I'm fine, my face is fine, everything is fine, Keir."

"I don't care about your stupid face, Dylan! I told you not to go there, I warned you because I knew, and you didn't listen, you never do! you could've died you, idiot!" Keir's chest was going up and down so rapidly. Is he okay?

"Keir, just spare me that. I came back, and I knew I was gonna do it. Your anger is a waste of time." This is probably the first and only time I saw Dylan this serious.

"Dylan, if you just- if you hadn't come back we all would've-"

"Keir!"

Keir let out a long breath. Pinching his nose. "What did you find out then?" Keir spoke softly, after a long pause.

"Nothing really, nobody said anything. But I do have this." He shoved his hand inside his pocket, and when he got it out he had a paper.

Keir snatched it, reading the paper. I moved closer to him to see what's the paper.

I'll take her. The defenseless one.

It was written in the same font the other two were written.

Their eyes immediately shifted to me. And I swallowed.

Defenseless wasn't a very nice way to describe me, Baron.

"I figured that too," Dylan said, resting his head back on his pillow. "I was on my way back to you when I heard Baron scolding someone, I stayed there like ten hours, nobody said anything, nobody even noticed I was there. But when I got out, like last time we were there. I went down the stairs. All the way to the main entrance. I thought no one saw me but as soon as I took another step to the woods, I felt a punch on my face, and let me tell you it does not feel good.

"There were three people, not much older than me, they hit me. So I fought them, all of them, Keir. I did as you said. They all fell, but before I left there was something in one of their hand. So I thought it was good information.

"And on my way here, I opened it. I only thought of Mirelle. I mean what does defenseless mean? Maybe because she can't fight. Or because she doesn't use a weapon."

Why am I always considered weak or even defenseless? Just because I'm physically not strong enough? Just because I don't carry the deadliest weapons. I can only get hurt while watching in fear.

Keir scrunched the paper in his fist, his jaw tightened, I don't think he's breathing. I don't want him to be worried about me. I don't want him to be anxious in any type of way. We're making progress and I don't want anything to step in the way. Because I-

"Then she stays here," Al said. She looked...mad.

"Till when? We can't just lock her here forever," Dylan answered as if I'm not even here.

I cleared my throat. "Let's...let him rest." I got out of the room not looking behind my back.

They waited for a while inside but followed soon after. I got outside the house, I might very well have some fresh air too.

Just when I was about to close my eyes shut and relax, Keir's loud voice echoed through the whole house.

"Mirelle!" he called.

And I thought I get to have quiet moments staring at sunsets, pulling the grass from the earth in absolute satisfaction, while the wind brushes the hair away from my face.

Well, guess what Mirelle, not for you!

"Mirelle!" He yelled for the hundredth time.

I groaned as I rose to my feet. "What!" I yelled back.

He came to view as he walked outside the house. "Can't you hear me?" he frowned.

I'm not coming home.

"Yes, Keir, I can hear you just fine, I think the whole world heard you."

He took a few steps towards me. He stood, fully scanning me, then swallowed. "He wants to take you."

I smiled at him, both to assure him and myself, "I'm aware of that."

He took a step closer. "You-"

"Hello, Mirelle!" Adam greeted as he appeared walking toward.

He had a scar on his left cheek like the one Keir has on his eyebrow but this one was new. And bigger. He buries his hands in his pockets from the cold.

"Oh. Hi, Adam!" I answered trying my best to match his energy. Now, where did he come from?

"Are you ready?" he asked as he stretched his arm for me to take.

I hesitated to take a step away from Keir, though he followed me.

"Listen-" I started.

"No," Keir said sternly.

Adam frowned at Keir. "I didn't realize I asked you out." He looked back at me, "C'mon, Mirelle."

This is pointless and I hate it, I'll just go with him now and leave shortly after, it's isn't a big deal. I sighed and moved to him. But Keir gripped my wrist tightly.

"I said no," he repeated with the same tone.

Adam raised his eyebrows in a challenging look. "Is that what you want, Mir?"

I let out a breath. "Look, it's...it's better if we stay here." I smiled at him.

Adam's eye twitched, he nodded and was about to leave.

"Wait!" I called over to him, "you can stay here." Keir squeezed my hands, so I squeezed his back to shut him up.

Adam turned back to me. "You want me to?"

I nodded. Even if I didn't.

He shrugged and pointed to Keir. "He wouldn't want me to."

I turn to Keir, trying to show the pleading in my eyes. He didn't as much as blink, his face is still neutral, he nodded firmly. I gave him a soft smile, wishing to brighten up his mood a bit, but still, he had nothing on his face.

I turned back to Adam to find him already smirking.

He walked to me, paused before me before he took me in for a tight hug.

I held my breath. What is that? I realized that Keir has already let go of my hand, so I had no choice but to wrap my arms around Adam, carefully.

"Thank you for letting me stay," he said.

I pulled away in one move. "It's fine," I nodded. "You can wait inside."

He nodded and with a smile he did what I told him.

I turn back to Keir as soon as Adam's inside. Keir was farther away from where he first stood. He looked at me with a sad simple smile. He must've felt bad when he saw that.

"Before you say anything," I started. "Do you want to go out with me?"

He shot his eyebrows up. "So you don't want to go with him and you want to go with me? Trust me, I'm sure he is way more interesting than I am."

"Is that a yes or a no?" I asked impatiently.

"it's dangerous, you know," he reminded me. "Something could happen."

I chuckled, "let them try me, I'll make them regret the day they came near those muscles" I tapped my biceps.

He sorted, then, his eyes softened. "And, I don't you think that was your line, Mirelle."

"Well, I- You-"

"If one of us is going to ask the other out, it sure is me. Not anyone would deserve to be with you. No, it's not that easy. I know this took too much time, but, well, I'm sorry. I thought you wouldn't like it, and then Adam came, and-" He shook his head, and took a long breath. "Do you, my precious Mirelle, want to go out with me?"

My heart is a mess, and I don't blame it because I am a mess. I smiled, "I would absolutely love it, my dear Keir."

His eyes shone like diamonds. As if a princess had accepted his offer. As if I didn't just ask him for a monkey, as if I didn't tell him I'd name it Keir.

My smile stretched on both sides of my face, I held his hands and ran. I ran with him.

We ended up walking in an empty dark street, it was lit by the faint light of the moon. Few cars would pass by, but other than that, it was the sound of our quickened breaths and the thoughts in both our heads that filled the silence. I wondered if his thoughts were the same as mine. No. I wished.

"Mirelle," Keir called, startling me from my thoughts. "I wanted to...thank you."

I frowned. "Thank me for what?"

"For everything. Thank you for...helping me fix myself," he said.

I only smiled to myself, not showing the actual dance I'm performing in my mind right now. A person is not changed by anyone if he doesn't have the will to change, though I fully believe a person can change for someone.

I get it it's hard to just let go of fear, it may be even impossible because no matter how far we leave something that hunts us behind, in one way or another it'll come back in different situations. But...I believe there is some stuff that's way more important than fear. I believe that there are people or things in our lives that deserve to face whatever it is that haunts us for them. And knowing I was that someone to Keir -even if it was for a minute- Makes me want to cry tears of joy for a week.

I turn to him to say something but the words get stuck in my throat. I planted hope in you, Keir. You're the one who took care of it way too well.

"You're beautiful," he mumbled, stroking a fallen hair behind my ear

I turned my head away.

Beautiful? Was he blind? What kind of beautiful am I. It's the first time that someone calls me beautiful. And I didn't expect that. Especially not from him.

I didn't want to ruin the mood but I have to fix some stuff here. "Are you mad?" I asked. "At Adam, You know."

"No," he stated. "Maybe just...never mind." He shook his head.

"You know, to me, you're a little more likable than him. Just a little though." I teased.

His lips curved upwards. "Is that so?"

I nodded but showed him how little with my fingers.

"So, what book are you reading now?" he asked as we walked beside a wall.

I chuckled. "Well, nothing really, kinda in a reading slump, but I do want to read pride and prejudice."

He arched a brow but smiled. "Classics?"

I shook my head. "I'm not really into classics but people say it's good." I pulled his hair and then left it for no reason. "Other than that I read what you write."

He smiled. "Want an autograph?"

I nudged him. "And I'm arrogant? you know, Keir, you really could be famous, but you know what you're missing?"

"What?"

"Getting me a monkey,"

He deadpanned and shook his head and mumbled something about him getting this all upon himself, and continued walking, though I could see the slightest smile forming on his face.

There's just something...I don't understand myself. I don't...or do I? does he? Oh, how I hope he does.

I always love it when he smiles, when he's sad I always lose my mind. and when he isn't here I imagine he's here. He's beautiful, in every way possible, and I'll do my best to let him know that.

And his hair.

"Keir, your hair-"

"Well, well, if it isn't for the star of the show herself," a familiar voice interrupted.

I turned around to see who said that.

Oh no. Not him. Not here. Not right now.

Jack.

He began to approach me, and I began to step back. It's almost like my body knows what to do once he shows up as if it knows what's coming out of his mouth and is afraid to be faced with it. There's always that question that keeps ringing in my head the same moment I see him. What if he's right? What if what he sees is the truth? what if the mirror in his eyes is the true reflection of mine. I'm scared of him. No, not him. He's merely a stupid weak human, I'm scared of his words.

"Who's that?" Keir asked, with a curious yet raged voice.

"A bad guy," I say.

I tried to pull Keir away to turn in the opposite direction of Jack, but he stays at his place, not moving an inch like a rock. Of course, he has to be stronger than me, who isn't?

Something in me wants me to wait and see what will happen if Keir met Jack. I wanted to know how he'd face my deepest darkest nightmares, I don't know if he'd laugh at them, or if he too would call me pathetic for taking Jack's words to my considerations. I mean look at what he's been through, and I'm scared of freaking Jack.

Jack doesn't see Keir, as he's covered by the shadows, I'm the one he sees, I'm his prey. "Keir, please." I plead as Jack gets closer.

He must have seen the despair on my face because he asked, "What did he do to you?"

Maybe he'd fight him. Maybe Keir would scream at Jack and tell him not to come near me again, maybe he'd show me how to fight him. Maybe he won't.

I try to push him away again, but it's like I'm moving a wall. "Nothing, just-"

"What did he do to you?" He asked again, this time growing angrier.

My brain screamed at me to tell him. Every part of me did. I trust Keir, I do with my heart and soul. So why wouldn't I tell him? He told me, didn't he? I'd give it to him, my fears. I'd give it to him and hope he'll fight them with the sharpest dagger he has. I can share my dark side with him, I will, and I'll have my fingers crossed as I hope he won't run.

So simple, and small like many other words, yet haunting like the scariest ghosts. "Bully."

His face was eaten up by the shadows even more now, his lips parted and he slowly looked at his feet.

"Can we please go now?" I asked him as looked back at where Jack was getting even closer to us. Despite all of that, I still wanted to leave, or so I thought.

"No," he whispered, it was almost unheard.

I let out a breath as I felt my eyes burn. I really don't want this to happen. Not again. Not ever.

Jack is now standing before me having a big smirk on his face.

Why am I only weak when he's here?

He grabbed my arm, with a sarcastic smirk on his face.

"Jack please-" I didn't have time to finish my words as Keir kicked Jack's leg; he tripped and fell on his back.

Keir took out his dagger, finding it quite interesting as he looked at it and held it to Jack to see it. "What do you think you're doing?"

Jack's eyes widened. "You- who are you?"

Keir looked at him like he wanted to stab him. Maybe he did. "No, that's not the question. What were you doing right there exactly? Who do you think you are?"

"I was-" Jack's words were caught in his throat. He looked at me with pleading eyes.

No. I don't want him to look at me. I don't want him to look at me like he didn't do anything like he didn't hurt me like his words aren't imprinted on my mind and are constantly being played on repeat. I don't want him to look at me like we're friends and I'm supposed to save from the monster. He's the monster. Now, I just have the power over him.

Keir gritted on his teeth, and the blade against Jack's throat drew deeper. "Why are you looking at her! Look at me!" He smiled bitterly and clamped Jack's arm. "Not the big strong boy anymore? waiting for the princess to save you now?"

Jack's fear was clear on his face as he swallowed, "I'm sorry."

Keir's feature's remained neutral. "How sweet. But you're still not leaving."

Jack stuttered. "Then, what d-do you want me to d-do?"

"If it was up to me, I wouldn't let your face be recognizable. What you did to her I wouldn't allow a living thing to do and live. You hurt her. I don't know how you did it, but I do know that I want to hurt you back ten times harder."

At this point, I couldn't help but let out a big loud sob. "Keir-"

Keir stopped drawing his knife further through Jack's skin but didn't lift his eyes stray from his face.

"You can stop." My voice came out so quiet.

His hands tightened on his dagger, his dagger in the process, held Jack's blood on its surface. Waiting.

"I don't want to see this."

Keir breathed heavily. Jack's eyes turned to me.

"Don't." Keir's voice was foreign to me, so dry, bitter, and revengeful. Jack's eyes turned back to Keir.

"Yes, he hurt me. Yes, I don't want to hear from him again. But, I don't want to see this, and I'm doing this for me, not for him. Please. For me."

"Mirelle-"

"Please."

He let out a breath, then his raged face returned and looked at Jack. "Never have I ever seen a person so undeserving of luck. If she wasn't here, I would've ended you." He swiped his dagger against Jack's arm, then punched him.

A sob escaped my mouth again.

"Apologize."

Jack swallowed. "I'm sorry."

"Louder," Keir warned.

"I'm sorry." Jack did as Keir ordered.

I don't know how to forgive him. Every time I try to forget what he did. it feels like the words print themselves on my mind even more. It hurts my heart. I don't know how it's even possible.

Keir drew his dagger back, rising to his feet, pointing a finger at Jack. "If I ever see you near her ever again, I won't hesitate to throw my dagger at you, even if she told me not to," he threatened. "Now, run and don't let me see your face again."

Jack nodded and stood and ran as fast as he could.

I gulped. "We could've just left."

He looked at me with a serious face but it seems he couldn't because his eyes softened, "I will not tolerate abuse. Ever. Especially when it's you," he stated.

I cried, "but you didn't have to do it. It was nothing. That was all nothing compared to-"

He shook his head as he quickened his pace towards me, he held my shoulder. "Don't you utter this word. I out of all people would know this, Mir. Your feelings are valuable, even if no one told you this before. What you went through wasn't nothing. Everyone has to go through pain no matter how, that doesn't make it any less important than other people's. You were strong enough to stand your ground all this time, you might have even been stronger than me for what you did there. Don't underestimate your feelings, Mirelle. "

He held me as I wept, it was the warmest of all the once, for this one I truly let go of all of these thoughts and memories that caged me, or at least I took the decision to.

"Keir, I still want a monkey," I said, smiling. Not for any reason really. I just wanted to tell him I was okay in my language. But yeah, I do want a monkey.

He smiled back, a true one this time. "We already have one, my dear," he said, sounding pleased.

What. okay.

Half an hour passed and we returned home, just to "see how the idiot is doing" that's what Keir said. Dylan truly had been through a lot with these people. I almost pity him.

His hair though.

Chapter 20

Keir.

We reached home at ten pm.

Adam left already. Good.

Dylan was fine, acting sick and covering himself with blankets, so we pitty him and serve him. I don't know how does a few punches in the face affect your feet to get your water by yourself but it's fine. Mirelle wouldn't let him move, and that dumbhead is living the life knowing that.

Al had a look on her face that would scare demons.

Dylan requested we all sit together to watch a movie before he dies because he feels like those are his last days. Because someone punched him in the face.

Tangled.

I have no idea how he's seventeen, and I have no idea how Mirelle is eighteen after she told him he's awesome for choosing the movie but I do know that I'm tired.

First forty-five minutes of the movie Dylan was miraculously healed and sang all the songs as loud as he can with Mirelle. When Al told him to shut up he immediately acted ill again.

They both slept halfway through. Mirelle resting her head on my shoulder. But I didn't mind.

I remembered and felt every memory and every hit. But Most of all I remembered the fear and the pain. Whenever I feel like I can't anymore I look at her, her beautiful sleeping face, that looked like a satisfying piece of art. I clung to her warmth, to the sound of her laughter, her whining about how we don't have a freaking monkey, and just to her. Sometimes I even allowed myself to lean my head on hers and listen to her rhythmic breathing.

She's...perfect.

That I could tell her to her face, in fact, I have no doubt that she already knows. It's the other stuff that I hide behind the curtains of my mind. I know she deserves to know, she deserves to know every beautiful thought I have about her. But it's me I want to shield her from. I can think of how I'd mock myself for the things I think of her. I don't deserve to feel such feelings.

I'm lost in the labyrinth she got me in, and I'm well aware there's no way out, I like it. I'm just worried Theseus would come and kill me.

Anyway, Al and I ended up watching the whole damn movie.

It was kind of good though. I mean apart from the part where Al kept cursing Gothel. After she was done cursing she said good night and went to sleep.

Such a sweetheart.

I turned to Mirelle, sleeping like a baby. Now I can't just leave her here, so I gathered all the courage in me and cupped her up in my arms, she was nearly weightless as I carried her to her room.

I set her carefully on her bed, covered her with a blanket, then stepped away. Before I fully left her room, I waited, to watch her again.

A beautiful sight indeed. I'd write about it.

What is wrong with me?

I walk out of the room turning the lights off and closing the door behind me.

I come back to Dylan, wrapped in a blanket on the couch.

He'll be fine.

Then I strode to my room. I lie on the bed as I think about everything that happened this day. It was rough. But there was good. I notice an orange-ish hair on my sweater, I take it. There was definitely good.

I'll have to do everything in my power to protect her. Baron knew she was important. And that's where I lose. I'll not let her live the fear I've lived, she deserves better.

It's not the end. I have hope.

That was the last thought I remembered before I drifted to sleep.

I woke up to a loud knocking on the door.

I tried to brush it off and sleep again, but it never stopped. So I dragged myself out of bed, having absolutely no problem in killing whoever was behind the door. Everyone was still asleep, and I'm not even surprised, even if the ceiling fell on their heads they'd need more than that to wake up.

I sighed as I opened the door.

No.

No. No. No. No.

Why?

"Long time no see Keir, " my uncle said as he stood right before me.

Let it just be another nightmare.

"I have to admit, I missed you," he grinned.

I just stood there. Not able to move a muscle, having difficulties even breathing. I'm pretty sure my hands are trembling. The world starts to black as I'm standing.

I recall every terrific event that has joined us both together, every word he said, every slap, kick, punch-

He stretches out a hand for me to shake it.

Why?

Why is he fine while I'm suffering? Why doesn't he tremble whenever anyone comes near him? Why doesn't he dream of fear itself? Why is he acting like everything is fine? Why me?

"Aren't you going to let me in?" He asked, cheerfully.

But I couldn't move, I couldn't speak. All I thought of was...

"Stop crying or I'll give you something to cry about."

"You are a big failure."

"Tell me what you did in your life other than being the reason your dad is messed up."

"Is it your mother's turn now? You ruined your father now her?"

"Don't tell anyone."

Leave.

I wanted to scream it. I wanted to scream at my head to shut up. I wanted to scream for help. But I couldn't.

It was like being in a cage, blind, and mute. Hearing nothing but yourself speaking.

But is it me who's saying all of this?

It's my desire that he's free, wandering around like he didn't do anything, like he wasn't a monster in disguise. He knows it. He knows he made me feel, like I was nothing, weak and pathetic. and I'm here standing before him scared to even breathe. Because he's got power over me.

Guess that's another thing to blame myself for.

He took a step towards me, I took a step back, shivering even more. Will he hit me again? Now that I'm old enough he wouldn't hit me, would he? What would I tell people? My uncle beat me up because I'm weak and couldn't stop him. I was terrified of the idea itself. I'm terrified of telling him no.

All I feel as I watch his wrinkly face is why the time didn't get rid of him already. I'm not supposed to fear my own uncle. I'm supposed to be breathing and smiling, yet I'm not.

All he did was consume me, I don't need him, I don't need that fear of him, I need to be free.

I heard footsteps coming my way, a voice calling my name, a soft assuring one that I knew.

But even her voice couldn't free me this time.

Not as I looked directly at the face who hunts me awake and asleep. Not as he stretches his hands to touch me. Not as his words rang loudly inside my head.

A hand touches my shoulder, I flinch at the touch. And the hand is immediately drawn away.

Mirelle.

I knew this hurt her, after everything she's done, now we're back here at point one.

He was speaking, but I couldn't hear him. I was probably afraid to, or just unable to.

Mirelle gasped, and I felt the realization hit her.

In a moment the door was shut in a fierce power. And his face wasn't what I saw, instead, the old wooden door of the house came in view.

I was sure I was gasping for air because Mirelle was using her hands to tell me to stay calm. I want to end it all. I didn't want to be that shameful.

"Easy there," she said, "take a deep slow breath," she instructed, softly.

I tried.

"Now let it out."

I tried.

"Look around you."

I failed.

And I broke into a cycle of hyperventilating again with my eyes full of tears.

"It's okay," she put her hand in front of her in assurance. "It's okay, try again."

I took a breath in. And let it out.

"Again," she nodded.

I was pitiful. A pitiful weakling, but I did what she said, again and again, and again. Until my breathing began to steady a little.

"Look at me," she ordered.

I lifted my tear-stained face to hers.

"You're beautiful. You're so beautiful. All of you," she says, her eyes glittering with her own tears, "You're loved, and appreciated.

You're enough. Even if you think you're not. God made you so beautifully, Keir. You're perfect. Just the way you are. You're-"

Her words were like sugar being thrown in salt. I wonder how she doesn't see the dumpster fire in me, how does she see anything- good in me at all, How does she talk believing her words as though they're true, as though I truly deserve this?

My eyes weld up again for her. I pity her for knowing me. I really thought I could make her happy, that I could pull myself together enough to have her.

When my eyes cleared a little, she still stood there, smiling at me with a smile that could light up the world.

I was still shaking, not being able to answer with words but with the vulnerable tears of mine. Yet...she seemed to understand.

"Who on earth is that?" Al asked, rubbing her eyes, as I realized he was still knocking. "And why won't you open it?"

"I can't," I mumbled with my raspy voice, looking at the floor.

Al stilled now as she took in my face. Her face became full of something wild, like a tigress. She moved silently to the door and told me to get to my room. when I did, I was surprised, Mirelle followed.

I sat on my bed. I didn't wish for her to see me like that. That weakness wasn't the best thing she could see me in. But I wanted her to see what's really inside me, I wanted her to see that I'm broken and not the perfect man in the world.

The mattress sunk downwards as she came to sit beside me. "I know you're scared and anxious," she started with a low calm voice. "I was too."

"Back in school, everybody would bully me. I don't know why. I haven't done anything. But they did it because they thought it was cool, or funny. I got scared every time someone looked at me. I felt like I was destroyed every time someone commented on my body.

"But it was a time when I said enough. I tried loving myself, thinking I'm just another beautiful part of nature. Like a star. Stars have different shapes and different colors, but they're all beautiful. So what's really the difference between humans and stars? They're all the same."

She now looked at me, lifting her head from the ground. "You're a beautiful glowing star, Keir."

"I knew my worth," she continued. "And I knew that there is no human who exists without purpose, or without being enough. No matter what they go through, no matter how life shapes them, they still remain humans.

"It made them happy, that I feared them. But when I came back again, knowing that in the end, it's what was designed for me and that I should be happy I have it, they thought the game wasn't funny anymore. Of course, sometimes I have bad days where I think, that maybe they're right, or maybe I'm really ugly or whatever they say. Or sometimes I get scared of them. But it is okay. I think it's alright. What really matters the most is the moments where I feel like I beat them, like I didn't lose. Even if somedays I'm back at the starting point."

I took a breath in. "How are you like that? You see life like it's the easiest thing in the world."

She now smiled, tilting her head to one side. "I never said it was easy. I just thought it's not bad. It's never bad life, it's just bad people."

She's too good for me.

The door threw open and Alana Stormed in. She blinked when she saw Mirelle but motioned to the door. "This thing wants to see you." Her eyes softened, "if you don't want to, I can kick him out, right at the moment."

I looked at Mirelle.

For her. I'd do it for her, and for all she did. "Do you want me to come with you?" she asked.

I nodded silently, then walked outside with her following me.

For the second time this day, I come face to face with him. All I could do was give him a grave face as my body did the things it does.

"Hello?" he said.

I didn't answer that.

"You're still not going to answer?"

Mirelle stepped closer to him, features sharp with danger. "What do you want?"

He looked her up and down. "I didn't ask you."

"You watch your tone with her." I threaten him, surprised with myself.

He raises his eyebrows. "Keir's got a girlfriend?" He scoffed.

He reached out to touch my shoulder, and I knew I'd freak out. But Mirelle pushed his arm away. "Don't touch him," she warned.

He laughed, "you realize you're just a kid to me right? What are going to do? Call your parents?"

She took out the damn kitchen knife and placed it to his heart. "Don't touch him."

How did-

He didn't take his eyes off the knife. "Where's your mother, Keir?"

I go completely still, everything just stops working. "None of your business."

He looks at me, his eyes carry so much that I couldn't read them. "Okay." He slowly steps back raising his arms in defense. "I just thought I could visit-"

"No," I snap.

"Fine." He grins and walks back to the wood.

Mirelle closed the door shut, I leaned my whole body on the door, letting my lungs get some air. Before she could speak, Al came from behind her. "You're worthy of breathing the same air I breathe," she told Mirelle, her lips curling upwards.

"You taught me, I shall forever be grateful." She raised the knife in her hand like a trophy.

Al looks back at me. "Are you okay?"

I nod. Looking at Mirelle again.

A glowing star.

From a distance I see Dylan waking up, then blinked three times, he turned to us. "I just dreamt I was a hamster."

The other laughed, and I proceed of thinking about kicking Dylan out.

But then again, a hamster's life is not that bad.

So I wished I was a hamster.

I have gone mad.

I go to my room, lock it to have some time alone, and to my relief none of them follows.

It was midnight when I finally felt a little better. though I still didn't get out of my room, not because I was afraid to face them, I was just thinking. and maybe a little afraid to face them too.

A light knock sounded on my door, and automatically I wished it was a particular someone. I finally rose to my feet, not caring about proving to myself that I'm not running. It was her.

Without any questions, I let her in. When she came in and sat on my bed, she scanned me, head to toe. "You're fine."

I nodded at her. refusing to take my eyes off of her. It was too late now to do it anyway.

"I got you a present," I tell her.

Her eyes shone with mischief and her smile reached her eyes. "You got me a present?"

I moved to my bedside table, opened the drawer, and took out the book I got her. Pride and prejudice.

I held it up for her to take it with a soft smile, but when she saw it she started jumping up and down. She took it-no-snatched it. "You didn't have to-"

I could feel myself smiling. I Let all that happened back there, in a dark spot far away. And I focused right here, in that moment, I was shaking, but I told myself it was just what my body was used to do.

"Mirelle," her name meant peace, prosperity. Flowers between the green of the grass. while I...I'm darkness in a person. Yet... "One day, one day I'll be worthy of you, and of having you, only you, and when I win over myself for you, I'll tell you." she stopped dead in her tracks. "I promise you that."

She swallowed. "I know."

Chapter 21

Mirelle.

It's seven a.m. I don't know what to do.

I walked around the house doing absolutely nothing for like twenty-seven times.

I'll go wake up Keir, that's an excellent idea.

I got to his room and just stood there, looking at him. He looks dead.

"Keir," I whispered, but he didn't answer. "Keir," I said as I shook him.

He groaned.

Oh, thank God he's not dead.

"Keir, wake up," I said as I play with his hair. "Is this a wig, or is it really your hair?"

"Get out," he mumbles.

"No."

"Mirelle, you can sleep here as humans do. Or you get out." He pulled my arm weakly to the bed without even opening his eyes.

"No. Keir." I pulled my arms away.

He inhaled deeply as if preventing himself from stabbing me, then he sat up straight, his hair messy and his eyes full of sleep.

"What" he says as he takes me in.

"Come buy groceries with me." I grinned excitedly so he wouldn't be mad.

He looks at the clock beside him, "Mirelle, for God's sake it's seven."

"I know right."

He looks at me like he doesn't understand his entire existence, and goes back to sleep, this time putting a pillow over his head.

I sighed. He brought all this upon himself. I poke his shoulder repeatedly, and rapidly as I order him to get up. In the end, he gave up and got dressed, and took me to the grocery store.

As he should.

The store was nearly empty, I mean I'm not even surprised it's seven.

Keir kept cursing himself as we walked. He's overreacting, it's not like I raised him from the dead.

I reach out to grab the Cheerios from the cereal shelf. But Keir takes it harshly and puts it back.

"No!" he snapped. And took the fruit loops instead.

What in the-

"You're not waking me up at seven, dragging me here, and getting the cereal you want." He threw the fruit loops in the cart.

"Fruit loops taste like unicorn puke!" I tell him.

"I love unicorn puke, it's my favorite thing in the world." He pushed the cart and walked without waiting for me.

I probably shouldn't have woken him up.

Nah, it's fun seeing him suffer, so I shrugged and followed him.

He did let me put a lot of other stuff though, but not the cheerios. I don't know why he hates them so much.

I went to grab something, and when I returned to Keir, I found him resting his head on the cart handle, probably trying to sleep.

poor baby.

I still woke him up again.

"Keir, look at that," I call to him as he follows me. "This cheese wheel is bigger than me."

He was about to open his mouth to speak but shut it as he caught something behind my shoulder. his face turned to the bored look he does when he doesn't like something.

I turn around to see what it is.

or someone.

Adam was walking towards me with a smile on his face. His face has healed a lot since I last saw him.

"And I thought it couldn't get worse," Keir mumbled.

He hates him and it's never going to change. I just give up. You can't make someone like someone else if they don't want to, I get that. I just want to know what happened for all that hate.

"Hello, Mirelle!" Adam welcomes, and shifts his eyes to Keir, "and Keir."

"Hi, Adam. Do you like...live here or something?" I give him an awkward smile. turning to Keir, who's knowingly glaring at Adam.

Adam smiled. "No, Mirelle. I don't live here, I just come here a lot since I live nearby, and well, I need a lot of stuff." He shot his head up as if remembering something."You left, the other day. Is everything okay?"

Keir answered in my place. "Yes, Adam, everything is fine we just don't like-"

I nudge him with my elbow. "We just remembered we had to do something, I'm sorry we left without telling you."

He shakes his head. "It's alright, Dylan and Alana was a fun company too."

I know he's lying. maybe Dylan was fun. but Al would never let him have a good day in her presence.

Keir takes the cart and goes to the milk shelf. But I followed, and Adam did too.

"Keir," Adam says and Keir rolls his eyes.

I nudge him again.

"I know you don't like me, but I mean you seem like you look at everybody like this. but do you even like Mirelle?" he laughs.

Well, if Keir wasn't already fed up, he is now. Because he fully tuned to Adam, which doesn't normally happen.

"The way I treat people or whether I like them or not is none of your business," he said...respectfully.

"Right," Adam answered. Looking at the floor.

I nudged him again. But harder. He winced but just kept walking away.

"I'm sorry Adam," I said glaring at Keir. "He's not in the mood today." I put a hand on Adam's shoulder, which Keir look at, and turn to the milk again.

"It's fine, Mir." He smiles at me., and I smile back. I don't know if I like him, I mean he doesn't seem at all dangerous, he's just a nice dude. Maybe we could even be friends. Or maybe I'll wait a little more to be friendly I guess.

I go back to stand with Keir, not just to pick what I want but also to see what kind of milk he got.

He leaned to my ear. "Would you mind if I punch him?" he whispered.

I- the guy didn't even look at him.

"Yes."

He closed his eyes, took a long breath in, and walked to the cashier.

He checks all out and carries the bag to the exit, when we're out Adam asks to help but I just tell him we're okay, so he takes my hand and kisses it, looking at Keir. Then he left.

Keir watched as he walked away. "I mean don't tell me this wasn't too much," he said, annoyed.

"Yeah, maybe a little."

He halts. "Then why don't you just tell him."

I sigh. "Keir." I take his wrist. "Walk." And pull him to the house.

We walked in the empty street, it was cold, the birds were awake. And the world seems just as peaceful as I liked to imagine it.

"My mom is coming today," he says as he pulls his arm free from me to take the bag I'm carrying.

I tried to cover my excitement but I guess I couldn't because for the first time today, he smiled. "She's excited to see you too."

We're not even there yet, but I still try to imagine her face. I wonder if she has black hair like Keir, or maybe he inherited her eyes. What if she writes too.

When we arrive, it seems they're both still sleeping. Because they are not outside practicing their dagger fighting. But there's someone, standing outside of the house, knocking politely at the door. when she hears our footsteps she turns around.

And she was the most beautiful woman I have ever seen.

The wind ruffled her brown hair on her face, but she tucked it behind her ear, revealing her beautiful dark blue eyes that complemented the sky above her.

Keir's mother.

She quickly walked towards us, or more like towards Keir. With a smile brighter than light.

She stretched her arms to her son but drew them back as she remembered. She looked at him with a sad smile, but love glittered in her eyes. No matter how much she wanted to touch him, she didn't want to hurt him with her own touch. I can only imagine the pain she went through.

Keir hugged her, drawing her close to him, as I showed him. He still seemed scared but I told him to focus on the person he was touching and leave everything else behind.

The beautiful woman seemed surprised but mostly happy, so happy, she teared up. She ran her fingers through his silky dark hair as she held her son closer to her.

If I'd seen this scene in a movie I wouldn't have believed there was such a thing. But here, before my own eyes, it happened. I have to say, if I was a painter, I'd have painted this on every wall I come across, and I would've called it "tears of a mother"

No matter how sorry and angry Keir had that father and that uncle, I can't help but feel happy and lucky that he had her.

Eventually, they both pulled away. Both their smiles are wide with joy. The woman wiped her tears with her hand and turned to me. Although my heart thunders a little. I don't try to hide the pleasure I feel. For her and him.

She approaches me. "So you're Mirelle, aren't you?" she asks with the dearest voice I've ever heard.

I nodded, impatient to know more about her.

She looked behind her back, to see that Keir already got inside the house and left the door open for us to get in too.

She stretched out her hand for me. confused, I took. And she pulled me in for a bone-crushing hug. And I hugged her back. I like hugs.

She smelled of lilies.

"You did what I couldn't do. And I'll always be thankful for you and what you did. Thank you. So much," she spoke.

I patted her back, and she finally let go. She looked at me with sad eyes, "I don't know why it happened, but it just did, out of nowhere. He'd freak out whenever someone came near him. And I didn't know what to do, so I just did as he asked and stayed away."

She held my hand. "It broke me. Every time I saw him and I couldn't touch him. But you did it, you helped him, Mirelle. And I hope you know how much he speaks of you, or how his eyes shine when your name is mentioned. Honestly, I wouldn't blame him."

She laughed. "He told me that he wanted me to come here, to show both you and me something. He wanted to show you what you did, and how big it is both to me and him."

I didn't know what to say. She says it like I did something I wasn't supposed to But what she doesn't know is, I'd do it all over again, I'd do it a hundred and a million times, and I would be the one to thank him for letting me. But I just smiled at her. "It wasn't just me, it was him as well. But... it's the least I could do, Mrs....."

She laughed. "Oh just call me Lauren."

"Lauren."

She put a hand on my back. "Let's get inside, I'm starving."

You bet. "Oh, don't worry I woke him up today to go buy groceries, you should find all the food you want."

She snorted. "Genius."

I like her.

She ended up staying all day, and for once, I found Al actually liking someone.

We both kept making fun of Keir the whole day, and that was pretty fun. He kept telling us it was not funny. But it was.

And she made us cookies, great ones.

When I filled my stomach with cookies, I sat on the couch to rest. Lauren took a place beside me wrapping an arm around my shoulder. "You know, Mirelle, I came here today for a lot of reasons, but there was one thing I had to make sure of."

"What is it?" I asked.

She shook her head. "Well, Dylan wanted cookies, so I could not tell him no. That was a reason, but you know what I noticed?"

"What?" I asked as I laughed, growing even more confused.

"I'd say I can see two sailors. Both of them are on two different ships. In the middle of the ocean, both their ships crashed against each other, and so their lives are in great danger. But thank goodness! there comes another ship to save them. Now, tell me, Mirelle. If you were one of those two sailors, what would you have done?"

"I...Would go on the ship?"

"Right? Now looking at the sailors, they can't get on the boat. And when you ask them why...their answers are quite odd. They'd look at each other dead in the eyes and say: I can't get on board. I'm afraid the ship can't take the both of us, only one of us can survive this and it isn't me. Mirelle, the ship could carry a hundred passengers."

I frowned, not really understanding. "Then why didn't they both get on board?"

"I thought you'd ask. They're afraid that if they saved themselves and got on the ship, then there's no way out to the other. They cannot see that the ship could take both of them, the idiots think that if someone won the other would lose."

"I...Lauren, I don't understand a thing I got a D in math."

She laughed again. "Translation coming straight ahead." She took two cookies, gave one to me, and took one to herself. "The two sailors are you and... -a particular someone- and all of the sudden the sea brings you together, and oh well, you're probably drowning. Then, to your luck, a ship arrives, and this ship can pretty much save both of you, it's big, it's forever, and it's love. But both of you refuse to see it because you're afraid that's selfish of you."

I ate the cookie more slowly, letting her words wash over me. That's not me and- yes. Yes, it is.

"You know, if I learned anything from my life it's that our hearts can destroy us or make us live our happiest lives, it's all up to us." She looked down sadly. "But I should tell you, Mirelle. That finding a heart is as common as dirt. But finding a heart that is close to our heart is as rare as a Diamond."

Now, I do not doubt she's Keir's mother.

"But how do you know the difference?" I ask her, finding myself drawn to her words.

"You don't. At this point, your heart is the one driving. And hearts are a blind mess. They are reckless and do not fear a thing. They might even take poison and mistake it for wine." She noticed my bitter expression and shook her head so quickly. "I did not come here to tell you a story, or to tell you that you're blind. No, but you must understand want you to want. Is he enough to fight for? to sacrifice yourself for? Enough to miss him so much? Enough to think of him even if there were a million around you? Enough to accept him even if he's full of scars and even if the time messed him up? Yes, these are the question to ask yourself. but the questions to ask him as well, if his answers are no, or if he didn't even scream a yes as soon as you ask it. Then think it no more, Keir or not. I'm telling you this as your friend."

I nodded and smiled, I didn't even know what to tell her, or what words would be a great answer to hers, so I just bow my head. "Thanks, Lauren. I really appreciate it."

She stayed a bit more. And we talked about other different stuff but then she looked at her hand watch and stood up. "It's getting late, I should go." She turned to the others. "Goodbye, guys. Dylan, don't eat all the cookies!"

Dylan smiled shoving one to his mouth. "Yeah, sure I won't."

And she left, with Keir following her. Minutes later, he came back. And sat beside me. "You're going to tell me what were you two talking about, right?"

I turned to him. "Yes, she told me about that one time you wanted to be Pepa pig when you were little."

He sighed. "Why do I even ask?" he mumbled. "Anyway, Mirelle. If it wouldn't bother you, please don't wake me up at seven, because I have somewhere to go tomorrow and I need my energy."

I rose my eyebrows. "To where exactly?"

"I- work."

"Don't act important, Pepa," Dylan called as he ate another cookie.

"Dylan, I don't know if I want to shove you off a bridge or putting the whole cookies tray down your throat so you suffocate and die," Keir said.

Dylan shrugged. "Can I pick?"

Keir looked at him like a mother with six children looking at what she got herself into. And Dylan looked back like he's the sixth child. Keir blinked and at him, Dylan also blinked.

Keir gave in and strode to his room.

But before he got inside, someone knocked on the door hardly and impatiently. Al opened the door and Jenny came in view. She didn't look as calm and happy as she does when she visits normally, this time she's gasping like she ran all the way up to here.

I run towards her, checking her whole for any injuries. She shook her head. "I'm okay," she pushed me aside as she came in.

"He's planning something," she breathed. "Something really bad."

In less than a moment, Keir was here. "Then what is it?"

"I don't know. But it's bad, Keir."

This is a nightmare, what he's doing to us is a nightmare. Doesn't he even think for a moment? that we're done with his business? that we're only just freaking children? His issues aren't supposed to be ours? I'm tired of this and knowing that I can't even run from it makes me want to throw up.

After a moment of silence, I could see Keir's jaw clenching and his eyes sharpening. "Don't go there anymore," he said to Jenny. "Stay home, it's safer."

"But someone has to-"

"We already know we're doomed. Knowing how isn't going to change anything."

She swallowed and nodded.

"Dylan, take her to her home," said Keir as he marched slowly to his room, his head to the floor.

I walked to him. "I'll go with them."

Keir stills. "Mirelle, please-"

"I have to. I wouldn't feel okay unless I go with her."

"It isn't safe for you."

"I'll be fine. Dylan's here and I-" I show him the knife I took from the kitchen. "I have this, so don't worry."

He doesn't look too convinced but he sighs and nods anyway. He sends Dylan a look-a hawk one- and we move.

"Mirelle I-" Jenny starts. "Listen...the guards they're-"

"What's wrong, Jenny?" I asked.

"They're not like the others. They're just kind and if it were for them...they'd have left in the first opportunity possible. They're truly my friends now."

I completely halted. "Jenny, are you out of your mind?"

"No! Listen, I know what I'm doing, Mirelle."

"You clearly don't, Jenny. You clearly don't."

Her face suddenly changed. "I trusted you when you followed a dude and told me I should just drop it, I trusted you when you went to their house again, I trusted you when I hated it, I was worried sick about you, but I knew you knew what you're doing. I spied on them, Mirelle. They are no harm. They're good people. "

I don't answer. I trust her, more than words could tell, but it's the people I don't trust. It's not easy when anyone around you could be holding a knife to your back.

"I'm sure they can even help us with Baron if we ask."

I only nod and link my arm with hers as we walk.

I missed her.

Keir.

Dylan and Mirelle arrived safely, they were tired. So Mirelle just said good night and strode to her room.

Dylan approached me and took the seat on my right as I took a sip from my drink and watched him. Dylan stayed quiet, and that's not him, so I knew he wants to say something.

"What?" I asked.

He suddenly turned to me and grinned. "What do you mean? I love you and I just want to sit with you."

"What?" I repeated.

He sighed and leaned his back on his seat. "I- just tell her already!"

I paused and set my glass on the counter. "What?"

"I mean come on! Everyone can see it. You're in love with her you idiot. So, tell her."

Is it really that obvious? I look stupid.

"I don't know Dylan. She's..."

"Yeah I know, pretty, perfect, makes me want to fly on a winged dolphin, all that love stuff. I get it. She gets me Doritos, Keir. No one gets me Doritos. She...just tell her."

I look him up and down. "Go inside. Why am I even talking to you?"

He shrugs and smiles, then leaves for his room.

As stupid as he gets, he's useful.

Sometimes.

Chapter 22

Keir.

I get dressed, brush my hair, put on my black jacket, and go to the playground Mirelle took me to before.

As I walked, people looked at me with an uncomfortable look, though it didn't matter. I mean you don't see a person dressed in black and looking like a serial killer -when he might very well be- every day. And I love intimidating people.

I feel a tug on my leg and look down.

Here she is.

"Hello there, Kayla," I said with a smile as I knelt down to look at her.

She chuckled. "I waited for you every day."

"I promised I'd come back, didn't I?" I tilted my head.

She nodded and put her arms behind her back. "Do you want to play on the seesaw with me?" she asked.

People are still looking at me.

Would I like to see a serial killer on a seesaw?

"Sure."

She sat on one side and I took the other. "So, Kayla."

"Hmm."

"Should I tell her what I feel?" I asked her, I think she's the perfect person to tell me the answer.

"Tell who what?" she asked as I push myself down to lift her from the ground; she likes that.

"Mirelle."

"Who's Mirelle?" she frowns.

How can she possibly forget her?

"You know, the girl who was with me the other day."

She rolls her eyes. "Oh. Her," she says like she doesn't care, but I know she does so I went on.

"Do I tell her?" I ask her again.

I came all the way here, brought myself a vanilla ice cream, smiled as I ate it because it made me think of her, and now I'm seesawing with the one I claim would fix my life.

"My mom always tells me that if I have to use the bathroom I should tell her and that I shouldn't hold it in."

"Well, I- I didn't mean using the bathroom, but that's helpful."

"You're welcome."

We kept on seesawing though, it's pretty fun actually. But now two little girls, not so younger than Kayla, came to me, "You're too big to play here, get down so we get to try it."

Too big? What on earth do they mean too big? I'm a freaking glowing star.

"Oh, you're mad? Go cry about it, you weirdos, because he's not getting off of it!" Kayla snapped back at them.

They seemed more scared of her than me, so they left.

"Don't bring Mirelle with you next time," She said, her soft voice coming back again.

Okay, there's a line and she crossed it. "Why?"

"Because she's nosy."

Right.

"I like her that way," I replied.

She gave me a look like she's been betrayed. But switch back to smile as I lift her side of the seesaw.

We kept playing for like half an hour more, and in the end, we both got off the seesaw. And I left after I said goodbye.

As I'm on my way home, I look at my feet as I think of alot of stuff, Work, Baron, what Baron could do, what i can do agaisnt whatever evil he'll do, how I'd protect them, I don't even know if I can. Maybe I'm not that strong.

I sit on a bench near the house. For a moment, I only watch the daylight, the birds eating with no worries, I try to live in the least of my fears. I rest in the beauty of the enormous trees with each leaf painted in a different paintbrush held by the great branches of it. I live in the peace of extraordinary things, if it's all so organized then my life could be not so different. Relieved, I rise and walk to the house.

When I was near home, Dylan approched. "So, that work was really important?"

I nodded sternly.

He snorted. "Well, Adam's here."

Yay. Fun.

"I just don't get why you don't like him, the guy is pretty cool," he said as we finally get to the house.

"Keep all the cool people for yourself, Dylan. I don't care."

And there he was. That annoying smile of his. "Hello, Keir," he smirked. I just ignored him and took the chair next to the nearest tree to the house.

"Keir!" Mirelle beamed when she saw me. Why Can't I just kick them all out and keep her? I mean it is my house after all. "I made hot chocolate do you want some?"

I smiled at her and nodded. And she quickly got inside to get it.

Adam stretches his back on the opposite tree of me. He's explaining the better blades you could hold for Dylan. But I could sense Al giving them an ear.

That's bad. Real bad.

Mirelle came out with a tray of her hot chocolate. And she handed one to me as she smiled and then gave the others the rest of them.

Adam approached me and I acted like I didn't see him. What does this man want from me?

I look at Mirelle instead, having a conversation with Dylan abou t...Doritos.

"It's hard, isn't it?" Adam says quietly. As he stands right beside me.

"What?" I ask, though I don't care.

He doesn't hesitate. "Seeing her like that, not being able to touch her or speak to her freely while knowing that others could do that so easily."

I stilled. "How- how exactly did you know that?"

He shrugged. "It's pretty obvious if you ask me, I mean look at how you fidget when someone approaches you, or how you grow angry when someone comes near her."

It's what I've been trying to do, not letting his words or what he does affect me, but somehow, a little of it always does.

"But you got this, man, this is all I have to tell you. try to do it before someone else takes it away from you."

"What it?" I don't hesitate and it showed my anger.

He darts his eyes towards Mirelle. "You know, the chance."

"Every time I think you're smart and open your mouth, you continue to prove me wrong. She is not a a chance or a prize to be won, she isn't a possesion."

"Jeez, dude, I'm just kidding. You always take things too seriously."

I took a sip of my hot chocolate as I eyed him as he walks to Mirelle and the others. He said something funny, they all laughed, but I didn't even know what he said. I was busy thinking about his words. Why would she even like me? I'm cursed.

Mirelle came and sat on the ground before me.

"What's wrong with you? You look like a dying seahorse," she asks.

How does she come up with this stuff?

Probably the same place Al comes up with her torturous threats.

"Nothing." I shrug.

She gives me a knowing smirk. "Keir, you're bad at a lot of things and one of them is lying."

I didn't take that as an offense. "It's just- your hot chocolate is pretty good."

She flips her hair, but I can see her blush. "Do you think I can be the next Gordon Ramsay?"

"Yes, absolutely."

She laughed. "I said that to Al but she just glared at me."

"Don't take that as an offense, it's just her language."

She stood up. "Yeah, I figured that." She extended her arm for me to take. "Come sit with us. If you like, that is."

I want to watch how Adam will annoy me, it's like self-torture but more professionally, so I took her hand, and followed her inside the house where they all went to.

When we got inside, Adam eyes our intertwined hands, and then he looked back at Al.

Yeah, that's right, sucker.

She leads me to the couch and takes a seat beside me.

Though Adam switched his eyes back to her. He noted every move she made and every word she spoke. But I just had too much of this, so I took out my dagger and reflected the lamp's light to Adam's eyes.

He looked back at me and I act like I'm just admiring my beautiful silver blade.

He didn't think it'd be that easy, did he? He maybe got some of them but his knife won't hit the target it was mainly aimed at.

Mirelle noticed and took the dagger from my hand and put it behind her back.

Great.

Adam took that as a sign and stood up to leave, looking sad as ever.

When he finally left they all turned to me. "What is wrong with you?" They all said in one voice.

I folded my arms. "What?"

"What?" Mirelle started. "He didn't even come near you, and you look at him like you want to murder him, and then casually attempt to blind him!"

Even my little Sherlock Holmes.

So I continued, "And what exactly is wrong with that?"

Dylan stepped in. "I don't know if no one told you but trying to take someone's eyes off is a crime."

I shrugged. "Well, I didn't blind him...yet."

All scoffed. "And what do you want? A golden star?"

Mirelle sighed. "Just don't try to kill him next time please, Keir."

I just nodded as I rose to my feet and took my dagger. "Will consider." I paced to my room.

Minutes later, I heard a knock on my bedroom door as I lay on my bed staring at the ceiling.

"Come in," I called.

The door was opened and then shut as someone stepped inside. And before she sat beside me, I knew who it was.

She played with my hair, curling it around her fingers. I just stared at the ceiling.

"Are you okay?" She asked, concern in her voice.

I sighed, surprised at my movements, I reached for my notebook on the bedside table.

I opened it and gave it to her to read.

"I'm in a cage, eyed by those who think of me as their amuseme nts.When I cry, they think I sing,I cry, 'am I blind? what for am I not seeing the colors in my feathers? What for can't I open the cageand fly to take back what's been taken from me?'What a shame must I be for the letters of my messenger, what shame must I be for them as they sit and watch me,unable to fight to get them back.I do know how to fight, but my hand is made of clay."

She turned the paper.

"He is a robber of dreams and hopes.He puts them in his bag and runs, not caring if they're someone else's hearts.And he dares to call them his.For whoever faces his wrath is either mad or dead.And my dear, I am both.So I follow him, to the deepest oceans of blood,to the darkest woods of witches,to the evilest fires below to set him on fire if I can.There, I would have never gone. for my fears would have eaten me alive if he wouldn't.But you, the painter of my dreams, the poisoner of wrath,my fears seem to forever bow to you."

I close the notebook and put it back. And then I turn to her, only finding understanding in her eyes. Which instantly triggers relief in me. She always understood me.

"Stay with me like this," I tell her, "please."

She unwrapped her arms from me and looks at me, with a soft voice she asks, "why would I?"

"Because I-"

"There's not enough reason for me to stay." She looks down. "I can't. Did you think that maybe I'd say no?"

"I did but-"

She interrupted again, "Listen, Keir. I-I pitied you. That's why I helped you in the first place. But I promise you now it's not like that...you're my friend and I wouldn't want to hurt you."

It didn't hurt. That's what I told myself. Her words didn't hurt, it didn't that just seeing her like that made it worse.

She was leaving, and I panicked. "Please." I stretched my arms towards her. "Stay," I whispered as she shuts the door behind her.

Fear rippled through me, and then guilt. And then regret. It was getting so tight that I couldn't breathe.

"Keir," a soft voice called. "Keir!"

And I jolted awake.

I found myself still on the bed.

"It's okay. It was just a dream," she assured, stroking my hair. "I'm here."

She's here.

I let out a sigh of relief. Yet something rippled through my whole body, I had to let it out. "Stay with me like this," I breathed. "Please." I had to caress her hand to convince myself she was real.

She sucked in her breath. "I will," she nodded. "I'll always be."

"You promise?"

"I do," she replied, stroking my hair with her fingers.

That was all I needed to hear. Because I knew then.

I'm telling her.

Chapter 23

Keir.

When I woke up, I sat up straight and ran to the shower, brushed my hair backward, and stared at my reflection. The scars outside and inside me. How can another person accept them?

Well, it's not the first horrible decision I've taken, I'll dare and make this one. I'll dare and hope it will be the best decision I've made. I don't even know what I'm doing, before Mirelle I would've thought any person who hoped was a fool, doing nothing but waste time on mere illusions they created to survive.

I am now the fool.

So I didn't waste time, I started searching for her in the whole house.

Outside.

She'll be outside eating Doritos with Dylan.

But...What if she left? What if I left? What if I wasn't enough? What if she just pities me? What if-

I love her.

There's only one thing I know right now. And I'll say it. If there was anything I could give her back, it's this. I'll pray to God that she doesn't leave, and I'll pray that I'm enough for her. And I'll try my best. I really will. I promise I will.

When I got there, she looked at me, and well, I'd normally talk or ask her what they were doing even if I know. But now, I was standing with no words coming out of my mouth, looking like a fool.

She silently offered me Doritos. I shook my head in refusal. She shrugged and ate one.

"Hey, move out the way. we're trying to regret all our life decisions here," Dylan said as he brushed me off with a hand, and I feel this urge to stab him.

I finally spoke, "I- can I- would you mind a moment?"

Who am I talking to? My manager?

She sighed and handed her Doritos to Dylan. He looked happy, but as she stood up from her chair she pointed a finger at him as I do. "Eat it and I'll dislocate your shoulder." Dylan's smile faded to nothing.

She finally follows me to the furthest tree from Dylan's loud singing voice, which he thinks is good. I don't know how many times I need to tell him to shut up.

But anyway, she stood right in front of me, looking bored as ever, also a little bit curious. She tilts her head. "What is it?"

I have absolutely no idea, darling.

My hands were sweating and my face heated up. I'm pretty sure I was also slightly shaking. I was ridiculously pathetic. I didn't know how to say this, I didn't know what to do. Do I tell her she's a good person first, I should probably tell her how pretty her eyes are or-

Screw this.

"I love you," I blurted. And my sweet mind brought back different scenarios of her rejection and mockery.

She stilled. And blinked twice.

That's Bad, right?

Then she shrugged easily. "Who doesn't."

"What?"

She blinked again. And then laughed. Like hysterically laughed. "I have a declaration to make too," she said after quitting the laughter a little. Wiping the tears caused by the extreme laughter.

My heart beats with hope. "What is it?"

She closed her eyes and took a deep breath. "You have nice hair." Then she winked at me like four times.

Does she want to kill me with a heart attack? Somehow I can feel it happening.

So before I die, I hold both her arms tightly but gently and I look at her dead in the eyes. "Answer me," I breathed. "Please."

I'm not some perfect guy like in movies or in her books. I cry, I feel weak, physically and emotionally even mentally, but for her... I can be enough. I fought for her against myself I'm sure not any knight in shining armor could've done it.

I tucked some hair behind her ears and looked down. "I- I know I'm shattered. It's so dark inside that I get lost there sometimes, my heart is scared of love. I'm a mess of everything life has made me into, maybe a monster, a stranger, or maybe that's just what I am. Yet here I am, telling you I love you, and promising you that I'll fight for you, and I'll try to be worthy of you, and protect you before I even think about myself.

"You believed in me when I didn't. You fought when I couldn't. You smile when you're in the middle of danger, you held my hand when no one else dared and smiled.

"I love you, Mirelle."

She stilled she tilts her head and a tear slipped down her face. "I love you. So much I can't imagine anything but us and this."

"I- I don't even know what to say. Every moment with you is saved right there." She points to her head. "And replayed every night before I go to sleep.

"I dreamt of this. Of you."

My heart beats faster with her words I was sure she could hear it from our proximity. It felt as though it was going to jump out of my chest into her, joining her heart with it.

"I love you," she answers back just loud enough that Dylan hears it.

Dang it.

"Al! Al, it's happening! I'm not kidding-" his voice faded as he got inside the house.

As for me, I was so happy I didn't know this was even possible. So I looked back at her. She blinked, but this time there was a smile on her face.

This is it. I got everything I wanted.

I won.

Dylan came back with his violin.

Dramatic fool.

Al came beside Dylan, boredom filling her face, but also something like awe.

There was too much happening too fast. I didn't have time to comprehend. Well, I didn't think it'd turn up like this. And that's my fault.

She wrapped her tiny arms around my hand, giggling, "I love you."

The sound of her words was like a lullaby. One that I loved, one that I'd listen to enchant myself every day if I could.

She loves me. She loves me.

Then Dylan decided to play louder with an even more dramatic melody.

I glance towards him, half glaring and half begging him to have mercy on me. "Leave," I demand. And of course, he acted like he didn't hear me and was just so invested in the romantic music he played.

Do I call him a doctor? Or a vet?

"C'mon Dylan." Al glared, "I won the bet, now come here or I'll make them twenty bucks."

Dylan paused his violin and sighed. "But for real, you didn't think Mirelle would say it first? It was just so obvious." He raised his arms as he followed her away from us.

Weirdos. That's what they are.

Mirelle looked up at me. "Did they bet on us?" she frowned.

I shrugged. "It's the least you can expect."

She laughed. The laughter I write about. "This is not all I have to say yet," she says and pulls away from my arms.

"Go right ahead."

She took a deep breath in. "Your hair-"

"Oh my Gosh, Mirelle. Stop it!"

"Interrupt me again, and I'll-"

I folded my arms over my chest. "You'll do what?"

I stilled as I felt a sharp point on my chest. I look at it. It's my dagger in Mirelle's hand.

"How did you take that?" I questioned quietly.

She smirked, "you're not the only one with talent." She pressed the dagger a little closer to me. "But now that we're all equal, I guess it's fine. That's for pointing this knife to my throat."

I couldn't help but feel my lips curl upwards. Was it pride I feel?

"Here I am Keir striker, the girl who would wreck your floating ship just to see you beg for my help, do you really want that for yourself?"

Now, she's scared of ants, so if she thought about doing anything bad, the worst thing she'd do is buy Cheerios.

But that was one line, so I'll play along.

"It would be delightful to beg you for my life, my love. It would be a marvelous sight indeed to watch a ship drown with you."

Her mouth curled into a smile, she took the dagger away slowly from my chest, putting it back in her pocket.

"I would fight for you in an ocean filled with sharks, in an alley filled with thieves. I taught myself to fight for myself so I could fight for you."

She smiled. "I've always known you were enough anyway."

She held my hands tightly and smiled. "You're not a mess Keir Striker, and even if you were, I've always loved your mess."

Stars were dancing on her face, they always did. Her hair had a shine like steel when she stood in the sun. I smiled at that cause I always loved it.

Time stopped, it was only her and I. Like rain and wind against the skin. A dagger clashing against a dagger. A meteor crashing against another, Only that it's her and me.

It was perfect.

Chapter 24

Mirelle.

It's been two days since Keir told me he loved me. And I told literally everyone. I told mom, dad, Jenny, the cashier guy, and even a stray cat I found.

Jenny came over and we celebrated, but Keir hated himself for inviting her because she kept threatening him about what she'll do to him if he hurt me, not that Dylan and Al didn't agree.

Anyway, sometimes I just wish I could put my tongue in my mouth where it belongs and not act smart when I am clearly stupid.

I asked Keir to teach me how to fight with a dagger.

"I just don't understand why can't we just stab the person and run," I ask with his dagger in my hands trying to follow his position.

He took my arm and lifted it a little. "One, you can. I'm just teaching you self-defense and fighting back against someone with a dagger who actually can fight. Two, you'll probably get stabbed first "

"Well, I've changed my mind. I'd rather die than move."

He gave me a look that said, 'shut up and do what I tell you.'

"I mean what is in life that deserves holding on to?" I said, trying to act like old desperate people.

"Me!"

"You're so self-centered."

I dropped my arm back from where he lifted it for like the thirty-seventh time this day. Did I mean to do it? No. But did I like it because I like annoying him? Yes.

He pinched his nose, "Mirelle, Darling. Dylan is enough torture for me."

Aw.

I lean in and pinch his cheeks.

He smiled and his face brightened. "Well that was sweet, but we're still doing this."

I facepalm. "Oh come on!"

He shifts his face back to the strict teacher's face. Which, if you haven't noticed yet, I hate to death. "Show me a drop point thrust," he ordered, and who am I to freaking object. I did what he taught me, which was by the way, pointless. All that for Dylan to believe I can do it. I don't even know why I get myself into bets everyone knows I'd lose.

"I hate you so much. You know that, right?" I tell him as I repeated the move.

"Everyone knows you love me," he defended. "Now repeat."

I take his dagger and strike.

"No." He walks to me and lifts my arm. "Don't look at my face look at what I'll do." First, he balances the dagger to what he calls angle six, then one, and then eleven. "Listen, you'll stop at three points here. One in the middle, then one a little low, then one high. The reason it's called a drop point is because you drop the tip of the blade, not just strike like a normal thrust. This one will cause more damage if done correctly." He leaves my arm and steps away. "Repeat."

This reminds me of that first time he gave me his dagger and was teaching me to aim. He was too scared to touch me that he called Dylan to help me. Now he clings to me like a lost puppy twenty-four seven. This makes me even more proud of him, so for that, I'll do what he says.

I hold the dagger as he instructed, and before I even try to do anything it slips away and falls on the ground beside my bare feet. I of course jump at Keir and thankfully, he catches me.

Dylan had the audacity to laugh at me. I tried not to mention that Al kicked him out of the house because I'm the better man.

"Mirelle, you can't even balance on your feet! Do ten Lunges and then another ten squats," he demanded, setting me on the ground again.

I'll drop point thrust him in the face.

"No, Keir," I said and bent down to grab his dagger and handed it back to him. "This is over." He looked so done with me. He also looked so good. And for what?

"Would you have the undeniable favor of telling me what you'd do if someone tries to kidnap you?" he asked calmly.

Call jenny.

"First of all, I'll slap him. And then I'm glaring at him. like Al glares at Dylan. Then I'll just keep annoying him and he'll hate himself and gets me back to here."

Keir arched his eyebrows. "Those all seem like considerable options but you'll probably be dead by that first slap."

Maybe, but at least I'll get to slap him.

I should probably slap Keir too.

"Now come on here, Mirelle. Baron has his eyes on you, let me teach you how to defend yourself in case I wasn't there." He had those puppy eyes again. "Please," he added.

How does he switch faces like that?

"I can defend myself just fine," I turned my back on him and walked to where Dylan was standing.

Suddenly, I felt my feet being lifted from the ground. I glance down, and somehow I find myself on Keir's shoulder. I began kicking him everywhere I could so he could put me down.

He didn't though.

"Alana, Keir's kidnapping Mirelle!" Dylan yelled like a child.

And I don't know why Al came running, but she did.

"Put me down you douche!"

"No," he simply answered. "If you're so good, show me what you'll do if someone tries to kidnap you."

"Pull his hair!" Dylan yells over to me.

Wait. that's brilliant. I go to grab his hair but he moves his head and gets out of my reach.

"Predictable," he mumbled.

How do I get out of a kidnapper's hold without killing him...or myself? Now that's something I'd google.

I just wrap my arms around Keir's neck to hug him. Peace is what this world needs. He stills and sighs then puts me down. I hug him tighter so he'd have no choice but to hug me back. When he does, I quickly spin and so that he's bear-hugging me now, I step on his foot, and then kick his knee.

He lets go of me and I run. "Weak! Can't even resist affection!"

As I'm running, I'm too happy I won, that my face hits a tree.

I hate my life.

I fall to the ground clutching my face in my hand. And of course, Dylan doesn't waste an opportunity to freaking laugh. Even Al snorts.

My head is spinning, it hurts and I think I'm about to cry. Keir picks me up, and I sense him holding his breath to prevent himself from laughing.

Betrayal can be from the closest people to you.

He puts me down on a chair. And when I removed my hand from my face they were standing right in front of me, Dylan was still laughing, and Keir and Al had faint smiles on their faces.

"You're all fake," I cry.

Keir loses it and bursts out laughing, "you probably shouldn't have looked back."

"I was impressed at first." Al shakes her head.

"Don't even talk to me!" I snapped as I walked to the house and ran to the room.

It was minutes later that they came and apologized, they all looked cute so I had no choice but to forgive them.

Running without looking is stupid anyway, I'll never do anything stupid again.

This is probably the stupidest thing I'll ever do in my life.

Everyone is asleep right now. It's midnight.

And I know that Keir told me not to go outside alone, specifically when it's that late at night. but I'm craving pizza, like now. Well, not just that, but I'm so done with having to stay at home every single day, so, even if I was scared a bit at first, I'll go out. Yeah, I'll sneak out. 'Cause really what would hiding do?

I take Keir's arm off of me, he doesn't do anything. Slowly, I turned to him and checked if he was awake, which he wasn't. And kissed him on the cheek. He looks like a baby.

I took my kitchen knife and left.

The pizza place is two blocks away, I'll go and come back before they even notice.

I walk in the near ghost-silent street and just look at my feet as I'm walking. The only sound is my footsteps and a few laughter sounds that are too far away.

I can't lie, I get scared. Walking late at night is terrifying. Especially when some random, mysterious people walk by my side. They could be trying to kill me for all I know. How much would I cost if they sell my organs? Probably like thirty-two Bucks or something.

I just pray to God they only want to know my order at the pizza place.

When I get there I order my favorite chicken ranch pizza and walk back outside.

That's good, halfway through and I'm still alive.

I take a bite from my slice of pizza and puts it back in the box. I should probably leave Dylan some, he loves pizza.

Nah, I'm hungry.

I only had to cross the street and reach the woods before I could walk back to the house. That was easy.

A hand grabbed my mouth, covering it to prevent me from screaming. They pulled me to their chest and put an arm over me to make sure I won't escape.

I try to fight his grip but he's holding me so tight. He doesn't seem to be so big but he is strong.

I drop my pizza on the floor as I'm trying to free myself from his grip. But he just stays where he Is, I bite his hand, hoping he'll take it away, but nothing happens.

Maybe I should've taken those lessons with Keir after all.

Wait.

I reach for the knife in my pocket and get it out, but puts it low for him not to see it. He begins to pull me to a van and my heart just speeds up more. I don't want to go in there. Whatever is in this van I don't want to meet. My whole body's shaking with fear and there's no one here to save me, there's no one to listen to my muffled screams. I'm just praying God will at least listen.

I try my best to stab his leg but all I could manage is a cut on his skin. He hissed and let go of me, and I didn't waste time, so I ran. But it was shortly after that he grabbed my collar and yanked me back. He held me right in front of him so I could see his creepy face. He covered half of his face with a scarf, and I couldn't see the other half regarding how dark it was.

He backhanded me, and I felt the blood trickle down my cheek. I could hear my heart in my ears as I sobbed, failing at all my attempts of escaping.

Suddenly, the guy's eyes widened, he let go of me and fell to the ground, clutching his side where a knife was there, and in less than a minute, blood was everywhere.

I let out a loud sob as I lifted my eyes to the person who stabbed him.

Adam was there, looking at me with concerned eyes, he took my hand and pulled me to him, and patted my back gently.

"Shh, it's okay now. It's okay," he said with a calm tone, I don't think I ever heard him speak with. He took off his jacket and placed it on my shoulder, as we walked to the house.

Keir was there, but a little away, wearing a black coat. Calling someone I assume is me.

"I found her!" Adam yelled as we approached Keir.

Keir whipped his head towards us, and- the hawk face.

That is not good.

He walked towards us and pulled me to him. He gave Adam a single look, Adam nodded and took a few steps back. Is that a thank you?

Keir tilts my chin up to get a better look at it, his thumb brushes away a streak of blood from my cheek. He's still said nothing. Just looked at the blood.

Should I be worried...or scared? Cause I'm both.

Maybe if I told him he looked good he'll drop it.

Keir then looks me dead in the eyes, his voice is quiet and like death itself, "who?" he asked as he tightened his jaw.

I swallowed and gave him a shrug. He looked over to where Adam stood.

Adam quietly took a step toward us. "I have no clue. He was just a guy with a scarf covering his face, and he had a van with him."

Dylan and Al both came back, panting. "We didn't find-" Dylan was cut off by Al.

"Where were you?" she snapped at me.

What am I supposed to say now? "I-"

"You what? Was it that hard staying inside the house? I mean it's not like you've been here for years. All we asked was that you stay here for a week!" she yelled, "we were searching for you! Everywhere, and I couldn't find you. Thinking that you're probably already dead," she scolded.

"Alana," Keir warned.

"I'm sorry," I mumbled, feeling my throat tightening.

"Sorry?" she scoffed-yelled. "Sorry for what exactly? For not listening to us? Or for lying? Or for waking all of us up to hunt for you? Why can't you understand that we have other problems to deal with? And all you do is be another one!"

"Alana!" Keir snapped.

I knew I was crying. And I knew all that she said is right, and that I also should stand there until they're all done scolding me. But I just couldn't. I ran to my room, wiping the tear and blood on my face with my sleeve.

I got to my room and locked the door. I buried my face in my pillow and wept.

I should've helped them more, should've probably just slept and done what they said. But I had to be stupid.

I want my pizza.

Chapter 25

Mirelle.

I cried. A lot.

I cried because I was scared of that guy, and because Keir was mad, and because all of them were mad at me, and because Al yelled at me and I hate being yelled at, and also because she was right.

But most of all I cried because I lost my pizza.

I don't know when I slept, but it was probably after I told myself I'm getting another pizza tomorrow.

And now here I am, awake by an impatient, loud knocking.

"Come in," I mumbled.

The door was opened and Al stepped inside. I watched her as she walked to my bed and sat on its edge.

Neither of us said anything; I was waiting for her to say something or continue scolding me, but she didn't say anything, I don't know if she wanted to say anything at all.

"I'm sorry," she muttered at last, still looking at the floor.

I nodded, not speaking a word. She was right after all.

"Mirelle, you have to know that we're in deep trouble right now. Listen, I've been there. He never let me do anything I wanted, I was pretty much a slave, just doing his dirty work." She paused and turned to me, "I wouldn't like you to be in my place, ever. I'm sorry if I yelled at you but you have to know that we all care about you."

"I know. I'm sorry."

She nodded firmly. "He really could have killed you though."

"Okay, we get it!" When I saw the slightest smile forming on her face I sat up straight and threw my arms around her. She's like my mom. She scares me but oh well bless her heart.

Minutes passed, and Keir came, his face still threatening and deadly, but his features softened when he saw us in each other's arms. He stood there for a little while until we pulled away. Then Al left the room, leaving me and Keir alone.

He came to sit in Al's Place.

"If you're mad-"

"I am, Mirelle!" he interrupted before I could tell him to get out.

"Okay, I get it, I'm the worst!" I snapped, "I said I'm sorry!"

"Where did you go?" he asked after a long pause.

"None of your business," I pulled my blanket on my face to go back to sleep.

Keir just pulled the blanket off of me. "It is my business!" he Yelled.

I'm either going to cry right now, or I'm snap thrusting him, whatever he said that was. I'm just done.

"Get out, Keir."

He let out a huff and pinched his nose. Dropping his head down. "Just- what do you want? Why did you do this to me? I lost my mind there, Mirelle."

"I don't want anything. I just- I can't stay in one place for a long time, and I hate staying at home for long periods of time. And...I just snuck out because if you all knew you'd tell me no because of Baron and all. But really I was just so...done. So I went out and got myself a pizza."

He stilled, and then slowly turned to me. "You thought I'd tell you no if you told me this?"

I nodded. "You're always worrying about Baron and what he can do, Keir. It's like our lives are just him. Can't you just forget him for a while?"

He shook his head and twitched. "I was not locking you up, Mirelle. I'd never do this. The point is I was afraid what happened there would happen because I knew it would happen, and I just...d idn't want you to go through this...alone. If you only just at least left a note or woke me up, I would have come with you. Really."

"You would?"

"Of course, I would! I'm sorry I didn't make it clear. Forget Baron, I'll never allow him to get in your happiness way." He let out a sigh. "You should've been really scared, weren't you?"

I nodded, burying myself into the blanket.

He stroked my hair, "it's okay. You're okay."

I wasn't scared of him, I never was or will be for that matter, if anything I felt safer with him, but my bad decisions wake up at midnight and I have no option but to make them.

The door burst open and Dylan stepped inside. "You yell at her again and I'll stab you!"

"You can barely stab a doe," Keir said tediously.

Dylan rolled his eyes and pulled my arm. "Come on, Mir. I won't let you sit with such bad company."

I pulled away from Keir, stuck my tongue out to him, and walked with Dylan outside. He led me to the kitchen.

Wise choice.

Al was there too. She glared at Dylan when we came. Dylan took two bowls and the cereal, then he took the milk and poured it, spilling some on the counter.

And of course, Alana had to notice. "Are you always that stupid or do you just do it to make me want to die?"

Dylan shrugged. "Maybe both," he said, wiping the milk with a piece of cloth.

Al sighed and turned to what she was doing.

If there is a word to describe this house, it would be chaotic.

I didn't complain though, just as I didn't complain about Al deciding to bang every pot in the kitchen, making an absolutely beautiful noise.

"Careful, Al. You're going to wake up Billy," Dylan warned as he shoved a spoonful of cereal into his mouth.

"You say it like I care."

"Wait, who's Billy?" I ask.

"Adam," they both said in one voice.

"Adam is here?"

Al rolled her eyes, "He's the one who came here in the first place. He said he brought Dylan the blades he wanted to see. But when he woke us all up we couldn't find you and we all almost lost our minds including him."

Good thing he spent the night here then.

"Why do you call him Billy?" I asked again.

Dylan put his empty bowl in the sink for Al to wash, and in return, she glared at him, "Keir does because he doesn't like him, so we both call him Billy too."

I snort. "Keir calls Adam Billy? Where is he?"

"We left him to freeze on the couch, I don't know how he's still asleep," Al said like the whole situation is just normal.

I stood up and went to check on Adam. The poor guy was sprawled on the couch with his arm on the floor. They didn't even give him a pillow. Or a blanket. They pretty much invented a new kind of torture.

Do I wake him up? Or leave him to suffer?

He did save me last night though, and he was pretty nice. I hope Keir's starting to like him. And from the way Adam is asleep, on a couch, in our house. I think we're starting well.

I slightly shake him, "Adam," I whisper.

He groans and shifts. Squinting his eyes from the sunlight.

"You can go sleep in my room if you're not comfortable here," I say softly.

"Mirelle, don't act like you didn't just kick me out twice from your room," Keir notes from behind me.

I jump. "Where did you come from?"

And at that, Adam wakes up.

"Good morning." I smile at him.

"Good morning," he said rubbing his eyes. "I should probably leave." He bent to grab his shoe.

"No, wait. At least stay for breakfast."

"I don't want to be-"

"Please."

He sighed and leaned his back on the couch. "Fine then, but I'll only stay for breakfast."

Keir walked slowly to him.

Behold.

"Thank you," he said sternly.

Adam swallowed and nodded, then turned to me and smiled, "it was the least I could do."

And then neither of them said anything. I might actually think this is the first time Keir talked to adam like he's a human, the first time he talked to Adam at all.

"Keir, if you don't feed me pizza today I might collapse."

Keir sighed and gave in to the fact that I'm not leaving him today.

Something exploded in the kitchen.

The three of us ran as fast as we could, I got there first. Thankfully. I might add.

Tomato sauce was covering every inch of the kitchen. Dylan -covered in tomato sauce- was standing right in front of the blender, and Al had a knife in her hand.

Dylan snorted, then laughed, "Al, I promise-"

"I asked for one damn thing," Al said with a calm tone, "just one thing. And you always manage to mess things up!"

Dylan wiped the tomato sauce from his face, then looked at me to help him. But I'm not touching him with all this sauce on him.

"Get out, Dylan," Al muttered, staring at nothing.

"You know you hurt my feelings-"

"Get out before I kill you!" she snapped.

Dylan ran out of the kitchen, still holding his laughter, and strode to the bathroom.

We got outside too. Then lost it.

"I thought someone was dead!" I roared.

"Are they always like this?" Adam laughs.

I look over to Keir, finding him faintly chuckling.

Aw.

Dylan got out of the bathroom, laughing At himself. "If y'all wanted to live you should probably get out of here," he giggled.

We all agreed and walked to the pizza place.

We settled in, and we ordered. I ordered my beautifully made chicken ranch pizza. Now I can die peacefully. And then minutes later, Al decided to join us, though every time Dylan spoke she told him to shut up, not that it mattered to him.

"I know you love me, somewhere deep down, I saw how you looked when I was hurt," Dylan teased.

"I was surprised they didn't kill you," she replied.

"Oh, C'mon don't overreact!"

"I'm overreacting? I mean why would it bother you? Our kitchen is going to smell like tomatoes for the rest of our lives just because you couldn't put the lid on the blender!"

"You didn't say I should-"

"I'm pretty sure everyone is looking at us right now, and now half of the place knows our kitchen smells like tomatoes," Keir said, looking around us.

"Yeah calm down guys," Adam added.

Al just glared at him, and then she glared back at Dylan.

"We can just get up and not talk to them so people won't think we know them," I whispered to Keir.

He did seem to consider. But our order came, so we didn't have a choice but to sit and listen to them fight.

We were done eating and then we left. We stopped at an ice cream place, I got myself a strawberry ice cream and got Keir his vanilla ice cream, which he appreciated, then kissed him, which he appreciated even more.

The others went to God-knows-where, so it was just us here, pacing around after Dylan made Keir apologize to me two hundred times for yelling at me.

"I think my head might explode right now," Keir admitted.

I laughed. "It's more entertaining to watch than a movie."

He chuckled, then out of nowhere, he took my hand in his. "Come with me."

I frowned, where will he possibly be taking me at eleven pm. "To where?"

"Just follow me." He pulled me after him.

We walked for about fifteen minutes, with Keir ignoring me every time I asked where we were going.

Could he be kidnapping me?

Before I could tell him to hand himself over, he stopped in front of a four-story building. It was an old one, if I was seven I would have probably assumed it was haunted by ghosts.

What if it is?

Maybe Keir was so done with me that he'll hand me over to the ghosts.

He pulled me inside the building without any explanations. I planted my feet on the ground. Does he really think I'm that stupid?

He looked behind him. "What is it?" he softly asked.

I gave him a knowing smile. "What's their names?"

He frowned. "Whose names?"

I motioned with my head to the building. "The ghosts. Katrina? Ben? Is it Billy? Come on Henry I know you're in here. Is Karen with you?"

Keir blinks at me. "You- what? Mirelle why on earth would I give you to the ghosts? Just come on." He pulls me to the building again. I cling to him as tight as possible so I wouldn't die alone.

The building was dark inside, though the moonlight coming from the windows was enough for us to see. the building was indeed old, there was a few old pieces of furniture sprawled around the house and a lot of paper on the floor. We climbed the stairs, it squeaked with every step we took but eventually we were on the roof. And only then did Keir let go of my hand.

I walked forward. The city lights were bright with colors, people were everywhere old people and young too. Everything spoke of life, even the cold breeze in the air said so. I couldn't help but shiver a little.

I turned to Keir to find him sprawled on the ground, his face facing the sky. Then he looked at me and motioned for me to come.

"You see that there?" he pointed to a single star in the sky.

I nodded.

"This...I used to come here a lot when I felt like it was all too much, I came and stared at that star, there wasn't any other in the sky, it was just here for me, shining alone."

He took a strand of my hair and twisted it around his finger, still starting at the star. "It looked like it guided me, whenever I came here it was always there, I'd cried, but whenever my eyes filled with tears it only glowed more.

"And I loved it. It was mine. Or at least that was what I always thought." He turned to me then, and I suck in my breath, because those blue eyes held the world in them, and I didn't hesitate to admire the stars in them.

"I never knew it would be in a person. I never knew this person will stand with me under that star, I never knew I'd be that lucky." He smiled and I couldn't help but smile back at him.

"So stars collided us then," I said.

He smiled. "It seems so."

He seemed happy. And I prayed for seeing that sight forever, for living in these moments forever, and for always feeling the passion I feel when I'm with him.

He was better than any book I read, or any quote I admired and highlighted. He was all the love poetry I read and didn't understand.

"I love you," I whispered.

"I love you too," he answered right back.

I hope this is forever.

Chapter 26

Mirelle.

When we got home, Dylan and Al were outside.

When we approached them they both looked...odd. Their faces were color-drained, both of them staring down at something in Dylan's hand, but Al snatched it from him and hid it behind her back right when she saw us.

"What is this, Alana?" Keir asked with a concerned tone.

Al looked nervous and disturbed, I never thought I could see her like that. "Nothing, you can go inside."

"What do you have behind your back?" He reached for her, but she took a step to the back.

"I said it's nothing," she repeated.

"Then why do you both look like that?"

They didn't answer.

"Give it to me."

Still, Al looked scared. "Keir-"

"Now!"

She took her hand out and placed it in his palm slowly.

There was a paper.

He opened it, his eyes widened, and he went white. I couldn't tell if he was even breathing. I came to read the paper and my heart sank to my feet.

Dear Keir,

I have your beloved mother.

You have three days to come, and give yourself up. If you didn't, I'll gladly kill her.

He dropped the paper. It was anger that filled his face now.

"When?" he yelled, "and how?"

Dylan swallowed. "When we came home we found it here."

Keir bolted to the house, and I followed him to his room. When I reached his room, I saw him taking his dagger from under his pillow.

"Where are you going?" I asked him.

"To Baron, I'm getting her back, and I'm killing them all."

He turned to leave, but I stopped him, and his eyes locked with mine. "Calm down, Keir," I told him though I wished I could say that to myself.

"How am I supposed to calm down Mirelle?" He sounded so...d efeated. "He took her. I wasn't there. He would-"

I held his hand, "I know, I promise I know, but you need to calm down and think before you make any decision you'll regret later."

He nodded and left like I'd said nothing, I still followed him outside.

"We're coming with you," Dylan asserted, following Keir. Al nodded too.

"No." He paced. "All of you stay here, they'll know you're with me."

He's getting himself killed. "But Keir-"

"I said no!" he snapped, then turned to me, and his voice became like a lost whisper. "Stay here. Please." He didn't give us any time to object and strode from the woods. I just stared at the empty place he left.

We were silent, but I wanted to scream, how could you leave him like that? how could you be so calm when he's about to do that?

I turned to them as fast as I can, I could feel my eyes burning as I opened my mouth to speak. but Dylan interrupted, "bold of both of you to assume we'll stay."

I couldn't hold on any longer. I fell to the ground, and couldn't stop myself from sobbing.

Everything was getting so bad all of a sudden, and I got overwhelmed by every idea of him getting hurt, and it was even worse to see him knowing that he could get hurt. Would I be selfish if I tried to stop him? Would it be selfish if I ran after him and begged him to stay? But...if he did stay, he'd be shattered. He'll hate me for it. I wish I could go, I wish I could fight. I can't. No one can fight as well as he could, but the fighter's always the one who gets hurt. No...no, he can't!

I felt a tight grip on my arm, lifting me upwards. and I didn't fight it, even if I wanted I couldn't.

Al was there, looking at me dead in the eyes. which made me cry even more. "Get ahold of yourself," she commanded, "if there's anyone who survived what could kill, it's Keir. It's either you come and fight with us like the fighter you are or stay here and cry."

I wiped my tears with my sleeve. "But he said-"

"Since when do we ever listen to him?" Dylan answered.

Never.

If he wanted to go by himself to protect us or if he was worried about us, I can't leave him alone. He always likes to do things by himself, without the help of anyone, but not this time.

Keir getting hurt is a must, Baron will make sure of that. But Keir, you're not getting hurt alone.

"Fine, when do we move?"

"Now," they both answered at the same time.

I blinked. "Now? oh okay, wait!" I ran to the kitchen and grabbed my kitchen knife.

I came back and we all strode to Baron's building. My heart sped up with every step I took to the building. My mind didn't stop thinking about the worst-case scenarios. I wonder how he is now.

"We're all going to die." Dylan decided to remind us.

"Yeah, but we already know that," Al mumbled.

Did they just agree on the same thing?

"I mean yes, but I didn't think it'd be that soon."

We kept walking until we were face to face with the building. Just the sight of it made me feel nauseous. Thinking about everything it's done to us, I want to burn it to ashes.

"How are we getting inside?" I asked.

"Like this," Al walked to the main door, she pushed it open, and every gun in the room was pointed at us.

Awesome.

She lifted her head high so everybody could look at her. Gasps and murmurs filled the room, but she didn't even flinch, she continued walking like she owned the place, like all of these guns were a bunch of toys to her. Dylan and I had no idea what to do, so we just trudged after her.

One of them dared and took a step towards her. "Alana Li?"

She still didn't answer, just looked at each one of them in the eye and it seemed like that was enough of an answer for them.

"Let us inside," she commanded, and if I were one of them, I wouldn't have said a word.

The room felt quiet. Not a single soul made a sound or dared to.

"Where were you? You're now a traitor, aren't you?" one asked yet he didn't seem so certain.

Al smiled a bitter smile. "Douglas, you're the last one I thought would ask such a dumb question. You know I'd never."

He took another step to the front. "Then where were you, Alana?" he asked.

"Somewhere that wasn't a prison."

Then, out of nowhere one of them threw himself at her, she stabbed him under his arm. Then another tried to throw a punch at her, she stepped away, twisted his arm behind his back in a strange angle, and put the dagger in his back.

"Anyone else?" her voice echoed through the whole room.

Silence.

She turned to the man from earlier. "Let us in, Douglas," she repeated her command.

Douglas looked at her like she's a strange creature he never saw before. "You changed."

"Was about time."

He looked her up and down, then eventually stepped aside. She didn't hesitate and walked inside with us following.

We got to the third floor quietly; no one asked us about anything. "Here's the office-" she was cut off by a scream. When we turned to where the sound came from, we all stilled in our places.

Blood was everywhere. blood spilled from men. Before I had the time to scream, I lifted my head to see who was the reason for all this.

Keir.

He fought every single one of them with a neutral face. Some of them were behind him, some were at his side. They were everywhere. He fought them all like all he wanted to see was their blood. He carved their flesh with his dagger and hands. He fought like a wild creature.

And I wanted to scream at him to take care, but he knew where every single one of them was. Men fell, and I couldn't tell if they were dead or not.

Dylan pulled me behind him but I could still see Keir. And his face was filled with blood.

I tried to hold myself from throwing up on the floor, but I knew it was going to happen soon.

A door opened slowly, then revealed none other than the monster, Baron. He came wearing a suit and tie, his hair brushed, and his cheeks red like he's having a meeting. Like he's not about to commit murder. He smirked, not minding the mess on the floor. "I expected you."

"Where is she?" Keir demanded.

Baron snorted. "Yes, yes, gladly. But you know the cost. I mean I tried everything with you, Keir Striker, everything. And nothing worked. I tried with your friends, I tried with the girl...what's her name again?"

I looked at Al and Dylan, trying to tell them that we should do something, but they were too focused on Keir and Baron's conversation.

"I am not working with you." Keir gritted, his voice was a wild threat echoing in the whole room.

If Baron was affected by Keir's words, or that he killed half of his men, he didn't let it show. Instead, he clicked his fingers, and two men came sprinting out of a room. They had Lauren.

Lauren looked a mess. She had a cloth covering her mouth, her hands were tied behind her back, and her clothes were either full of dust or blood. Her eyes widened as she took in her son, and for the first time, it was grief on her face.

She struggled between the guard's arms as she screamed, "Keir! Keir!" Her voice didn't come out so clear regarding the cloth on her mouth though I know everyone in the room heard her. "Please take me and not him!" It broke me to hear her words being yelled out carrying that much pain but I know it broke Keir ten times more.

It took everything in me to not run to her and try my best to get her out of here.

Keir forced his eyes back to Baron. "H-how? How did you find her?"

Baron shrugged. "You didn't think that visit from your uncle was random?" He tilted his head to the side. "I had to make sure she's that important to you. And well, money's is money."

I wondered why he came that day, I kept thinking of it till I drifted to sleep. But I don't thinkI could've ever thought that he worked with Baron. I knew for sure that he was horrible for what he did. But...I didn't think he'd humiliate himself that much.

Yet I still blame myself for it.

Keir gulped, and I could see it in his eyes too, blood from his face fell on the floor.

blood that wasn't his own.

I closed my eyes shut trying not to focus on that subject, and then slowly turned to Alana. "What are we going to do?" I whispered to her.

She held out a finger, gesturing that I should keep quiet. So I turned once again to Keir.

"I had to distract you, I made you think it's the girl with that paper I made sure you delivered. When in reality, I was planning on her all along." He moved his head to Lauren.

Keir's eyes drifted to his mother. "Let her go."

Baron took a step towards Keir but Keir wasn't concerned; he stood his ground without moving a step.

"Stay and serve me. And I'll let her go."

Keir eyed Baron. "I beg to differ." Keir didn't let Baron comprehend as he jabbed for Baron's wrist, in the same place I stabbed him in, and stabbed him again.

Baron hissed in pain as he took a few steps back.

"You don't know all my moves after all." Keir gave him a crooked smile.

"Get him!" Baron spat to his men.

None of them moved as they eyed the dead men and their blood on the floor, which made Baron ever angrier, apparently. "If you survived now I'll kill each one of you later."

One jabbed for Keir, throwing himself at him. He had a gun.

Keir sprinted, and kicked his hand in some way that the guy was left unarmed, he yanked his hair and stabbed him.

I swallowed a gag.

It looked easier in movies.

I maybe know now why Keir wanted me to stay at home.

He continued to fight as his mother watched with a horrified expression on her face. But it was not only fear she held in her eyes, no, she was hurt. She was badly hurt.

I tried to convince myself that I was not scared, that blood didn't affect me in the slightest, that seeing the one I love bloodied and fighting like that is not a concern. But I couldn't help my shaky hands and my racing heart.

"Move!" Baron yelled to all of them.

Suddenly, all the men in the room approached Keir with a weapon on them, they circled him like he's the prey they've been looking for.

I found my body running for him, not knowing what to do exactly. But a hand grabbed my shoulder and yanked me back behind the wall.

"Stay here," Dylan ordered as he and Al took out their daggers.

"Dylan, you can't-"

"They're going to kill you, Mirelle. And they won't hesitate."

"They're going to kill you too," I whispered-yelled.

"We know how to deal with it." He stared into my eyes. "Stay here and hold your knife closest to you, try your best to hide it."

After they both explained where I should stab someone to kill them they left on their tiptoes.

Not like I could do it anyway, even if I could, I'd never in my life do it.

"Hey, Baron!" Al finally yelled.

All the room turned to her, all their eyes as big as saucers, even Keir. "I will end you."

Baron seemed...disturbed by her presence. And for that, with only a nod, everything went to chaos, red.

Chapter 27

Keir.

I wanted to be mad at them. Wanted to yell at them for not listening to me. I also wanted to thank them. I was scared for them and worried about them. But I had no chance to do anything. They just showed up out of nowhere.

"Where's Mirelle?" I asked Dylan with the lowest voice I could manage as he punched someone in the jaw and knocked him out. I pulled him to the back so he could have a further distance from the man approaching.

Dylan smiled innocently, "Mirelle? Who is she?-"

"Dylan!" I glared.

"She- she's feeding her monkey."

He screwed up.

I was about to speak again but I felt a presence behind my back, I whirled as fast as I can, but stopped, startled at what I saw.

The man in front of me didn't seem as old as the others, I'd say he's twenty-something. But that wasn't what stopped me. The guy had two daggers in his hands.

I remembered my tutor telling me that a duel fighter isn't in my favor. But I was going to fight him, and fight him till he draws his last drop of blood like all who dared to face me.

The dual fighter has a bigger chance at distracting you, focus on their blades. Start with it yourself.

I eyed them and expected all his attacks, and with that, I planed my defenses and my attacks.

I leaped forward, speeding towards him, and aware of every step I took. I hurled my dagger near his neck. He dodged it easily.

"The Keir Striker. Is that all you got? I thought you'd be wiser," the guy scolded.

Never waste time speaking in combat.

He made a smart move and crouched low. I felt the pain in my calf before I saw him.

He didn't keep his position as he stood up again, "I have to admit I thought you're going to be as easy as your girlfriend?"

What?

I tried to focus on the fact that I'm fighting instead of who I'm fighting and calm down-

"You didn't know? I wasn't really going to take her. I was just distracting you before- someone stabbed me. And guess what...here I am."

I knew what he's doing. He's distracting me without using any techniques. And I know I shouldn't think about it. So I take a deep, careful breath in.

We faced each other, the look on our faces was like a challenge, or maybe we were just busy predicting each other's next moves.

A chess game, but make it violent.

Every move was like a dance, every action had a comeback to it, even the slightest breath could tell what a person is planning to do.

I planted my feet on the ground, staring at the knives: my true opponents.

I didn't give him a chance to act as I circled him and hit his knee so hard he fell. He pulled my leg so I fell on my back.

Expected.

He lunged for my shoulder with his dagger but I rolled and his knife struck nothing but air.

I stood up again, which was a mistake, but it was worth my plan. The guy lunged for another thrust on my left calf, and I tried my best not to let my face show the pain. Then he rose to his feet.

I thought it wasn't going to be this easy.

I swept my right leg wide, which succeeded in knocking the guy off balance. Here he is.

I shot to my feet and shoved my blade at his back, leaving his knives in his hand

It's a dishonor to fight a disarmed guy, but a privilege to win over an armed one.

I stared at him, as his eyes dropped the last drop of life in them, and his blood coated the floor.

He's dead.

A part of me was happy I won, and for teaching him what happens when he touches her. The other was scared, scared of the sight, and scared of myself.

It seemed like I was a ruthless, unmerciful killer. And I could see it in the people standing right before me, but I couldn't help but dread every cut I caused on anyone. But that's what I always wanted, wasn't it? To be feared so no one can hurt me. I may be feared, but it still hurts. Why doesn't it work?

I turned to where Dylan was, I sighed in relief as I saw both of them still on their feet, fighting. They had small cuts all over their bodies though, but it was nothing too big.

I searched for my mother, she wasn't where I last saw her. Instead, she was taken away from all of the fighting. And I thanked God she didn't have to see me like this; a monster.

But there's still something.

I approached Al as carefully as I could, watching my back, and hers. "Where is she?" I asked her in a whisper.

She looked at me in a knowing look but then averted her eyes away, like she couldn't bear it.

"S-safe," she struggled.

"How safe exactly?"

"Safe enough."

Why are they both like this?

What do they think I am? A fool? I'm already in a mess I don't have time to guess what they mean. I try and persuade myself that she should be okay, but the worry never shuts up.

"Answer my question, Alana!" I gritted.

She drifted her eyes to me. "She's okay," she said firmly and swayed to the left so she leads the man coming towards us.

I wasn't fully convinced, but I let it go because if I didn't I'll get myself killed, and I know she wouldn't like that.

We were outnumbered when we first started, now there are only two of his men on their feet, one of them was masked for some reason.

Alana was fighting the other, he slashed her arm, and so she slashed his face. He took a few steps back and she didn't hesitate to strike him in his stomach.

I turned to the masked one, but he wasn't anywhere in sight.

"What else?" I called to Baron. "Continue to hide and let your men fight in your place and I'll just kill them all," I said, trying my best to hide any emotions on my face.

He smirked. "I'm impressed," he admitted, "Leo was one of my best men in fighting like that." He motioned to the guy who had two daggers, he didn't even act affected by his death. "But that only makes me want you even more Keir."

Al stepped out to answer him but he turned his head to the wall on the right. "No? Well, how about this?"

At first, there was nothing. It was just a wall. I looked at Dylan to find him already looking at Al like he's seen a ghost and Alana didn't look so much different.

Then she came in view.

She was looking at me with apologetic eyes, not caring about the knife on her throat by the masked guy.

I fluttered my eyes to him. "Let her go," I said with a low tone.

But nothing happened more than his hand trembling with the knife against her throat.

I took a step, nearing them. But Baron objected, "C'mon...take it off, Adam."

And here it is.

Mirelle's eyes widened as Adam took off his mask, she looked up at him with a hurt look. Her eyebrows frowned and her eyes reddened, she was trying not to cry.

He threw his mask on the floor, smiling numbly yet still his eyes carried tears. "Here, father. Isn't that what you wanted? I did it. Am I a worthy son after all?"

From beside me, I could feel both Al and Dylan go stiff beside me.

He thinks he double-crossed us, but that's what he doesn't know. His knife missed the target it was mainly aimed at.

"I knew it," I mumbled at Baron. "You really think sending your son over will break me? I knew since the first day. Yet you failed in knowing anything you wanted to know, didn't you? I made sure of it."

Adam eyed me, his lips wobbling and his face was weak. When I begin to feel bad for him I shift my eyes back at her. She was crying.

"How did you-" Baron startles.

"How Did I know? Call it a curse or a blessing but I don't trust anyone that easily, when I found out he became invested with us I had to know who he is."

Baron was mad, and he didn't make an effort to hide it. "You're a failure!" he snapped to his son.

Adam looked at the floor, hiding his face from his father.

"And you!" Baron pointed an accusation finger at me. He grabbed me by the collar, "Who do you think you are? Do you really think you have an opinion? You defeated my son, my well-trained son, you fought him and won like he's nothing!"

"And whose fault is that?" I spat.

"If you're so great stay here and serve me!" he said like it's the easiest to do.

"I won't-"

"Over my dead body!" Mirelle yelled, and everyone else's eyes were on her.

No.

Baron's eyebrow's raised as his attention shifted to Mirelle, "oh." He looked at one of his guards. "Very well then."

I ran, without thinking, without a plan, nothing like any calculated moves I made when I fought.

I was so fast nobody had the time to act, I gripped her arm pulling her to me, and making sure the knife in Adam's hand didn't touch her.

And I knew this was probably wrong, this shows my weakness and allows them to strike, but I couldn't just stand there. Even if this was wrong, she's here now. With me. And that made it better.

In less than a moment, Al and Dylan were standing in front of her.

"Keir, I'm sorry I-" she whispered but I could hear the rasp in her voice.

"It's okay. It's okay," I said soothing her hair to the back. "Stay here."

Baron eyed Adam. "Kill. Her," he seethed.

"Go ahead and try. Show me!" Al snapped back.

Baron ignored her, he didn't even lift his eyes from his son. "Kill her and let's see if there's any hope for redemption left in you."

I could feel Mirelle shivering under my grip.

"Father-" Adam pleaded.

"What?" Baron snapped.

Adam looked at us, all the dread and regret showing on his face as if begging us to do something, but that hardly mattered to me.

"Take your knife Adam and fight like a man."

Adam shook his head. "I can't, I can't do it."

Baron looked at him with such hatred and rage. "Do it, or you know what I'll do."

Adams's eyes quickly shifted to Baron. "No," he breathed, "Please."

"Then do it."

Adam repositioned his dagger in his hand and looked at...me.

He mouthed an 'I'm sorry.' and continued to walk near me.

Let him, let him try and lay a finger on her and I'll break him whole. I'll make him wish he never saw my face in the first place.

"Fight him!" Baron snarled.

Adam gulped, and slowly drew his dagger, and raised it to me.

He wants me to fight him? I will. I've always wanted to do it. Always wanted to make him grief for all he's caused.

I lept forward, his dagger clashed weakly against mine. I continued to strike and attack with techniques I never thought I could manage. But he just dodged, weakly. It's like he wanted it to be like that. He wanted me to attack him and win, but I wouldn't let him have it that easy. Even if he wished that I'd kill him, he's going to fight for it.

We stopped when a loud noise came from the stairs, like a hundreds of feet stepping just to make that sound.

I looked at Mirelle behind Dylan, smiling.

Before I could ask about anything, about twenty guards came sprinting down the stairs. All their faces were angry and searching for something.

Then, when they were all fully descended, Jenny Hansen came in view smiling back at Mirelle.

Chapter 28

Keir.

"We're done with you," one of the men spat at Baron.

Baron had men standing with him, but the majority stood against him. I didn't know if they stood with us though.

Baron seemed shaken. "You- you traitors!" he roared. He turned to where Jenny stood and I could feel Mirelle shift under my arm. "I'm going to kill you."

"I was never with you to betray you. And about killing me, I think everyone here knows you can't do it. Oh wait, why won't you make someone do it for you?"

The men cheered in agreement.

"You're all words! All you do is pretend you're not a coward!" one of the young ones shouted.

Baron took a step to the back. "You want a fight? I'll give it to you! But don't come begging for your lives and cry to me when I put you back in your places."

Then it started.

Men shouted and blood sprawled, I couldn't even see who was fighting who.

Mirelle was shivering. And that reminded me of myself, how scared I was, and how she was there for me. I held her head against my chest as I tried to defend us both against anyone who came near us.

"I am sorry-"

"Don't," she cut me. "Don't apologize, I came here by choice."

That's stupid. I wanted to tell her, but instead, I pulled her tighter to me. "I know you're scared-"

"Of you? No. Never."

"Are you sure?" I pressed.

"...Yes!" She gripped my shirt tighter and buried her face in it deeper if that was even possible.

The room became suspiciously quiet. And I couldn't comprehend it. Not before I heard its sound, not as the gunshot thundered in the whole room that no one dared to speak.

Pain spread in my whole arm, but I could see the bullet in my upper arm. I fell, losing hold of both my dagger and Mirelle.

My head throbbed with pain, and I felt nothing more than shock. That wasn't what bothered me. Before I could reach for Mirelle again a hand gripped her arm and yanked her to the right.

I pressed my wound and took the dagger and didn't waste time as I rose to my feet, my head swayed in the process. But that was hardly the problem.

I forced my head to the right. A man had Baron on his knees with a gun pointed at his head, one of the guards that were with Jenny. But Mirelle...

No. Please, no.

She was sitting in the same position as Baron but instead, one of Baron's men had a big knife against her throat. Horror filled her eyes as she looked back at me. And I bet I wasn't any better.

"Alana!" I yelled at her, desperately.

But she had nothing to do. She looked back at me with a panicked looked. Then, just then, did she turn around and took a glance at Adam, she kicked the back of his knees and he fell, and like that, she placed her dagger on his throat.

Alana

She was a tigress.

A fighter by all means. Life's made a mess of her, but she's always thought mess was another image of art.

She's never held a dagger against someone she knows or likes with the intention of harming him.

But that's how it goes. She guessed.

How it broke her to see a person she trusted and welcomed betray her like that, how it hurts her to know who he was.

Because she cares. She always has. So intensely and deeply, she'd give up anything for someone she cares for. It's just that people always knew how to hurt her when she showed it, so she decided to hide.

With every bad look she gave to someone, she always hid love and affection beneath, she buried deep down that people acted like it was not even here. So she decided to act like it too.

That's how she felt when she held the dagger to that boy she thought was her friend felt like. A loss.

And it hurt her, even more, to look at Mirelle, the sister that was like a gift given freely to her. And it broke her heart to a thousand pieces when she looked back at Keir with his pleading eyes.

She nearly begged him to assure her it was going to be fine like he always did. She wanted him to tell her to keep fighting.

But is it a shame if her arms hurt so much that she can't anymore?

She tried to focus on the terrified Mirelle in front of her, to think of what the boy under her arm had done to them. How he hurt her friends, manipulated them, and made them think he was to be trusted. She tried to hate him. But all she felt was sadness, and anger at herself.

"I'll kill him!" she yelled, looking at the monster himself in the eyes. "Lay a hand on her and I'll kill him!"

Baron smiled at her, he always did that when she's mad. as if he's mocking a child. "Alana, It's been a while. I've missed you."

She didn't let any of his words get through her. "Let her go," she spat as if even talking to him was like poison on her tongue.

He shook his head, "I can't."

She swallowed and convinced herself she was not about to collapse. "Why?" she let out. "Why all of this?"

It's the question she has always asked herself.

Baron laughed, and Alana wondered if he's gone mad. "Because I simply can. I won't watch power go to waste and fold my arms as I watch. This is how I die, Alana, with always having the better in everything. This is how I won't be forgotten and wasted like I've done nothing." He then stopped and looked her dead in the eyes. "If there's anything you'll learn from me, Alana, is that power never dies."

If he was someone else she would probably have listened. If he was her father who told her that, she would've listened because she only saw him as one who has got power over her. But if she really was taught anything in her short life, it was that all power is nothing but an illusion, a trick. Most likely made to curse you.

"Let her go," she said, exhausted.

Baron appeared to move towards her on his knees but was instantly held back by the man grasping him. "Why?"

Was she really going to have this conversation?

"Because-"

"You love her? Or is it because he loved her? Haven't I told you that love was stupid? That it's weak and useless. And will only bring you to your end?"

Baron wasn't only the horrible thug that abused her and never talked to her. Baron sometimes asked her how her day was going, even once she was ill and he showed up for her. One day he'll send her to kill someone and the other he'd act like a father. But Alana knew better than confusing both. He was an abuser. That's what mattered.

She didn't want to talk, she stood on her feet for so long she wanted to collapse. "Because if you didn't, I'll kill him," she threatened, holding the knife to Adam's throat.

He shrugged. "Kill him, why do I care?"

Adam laid his head low; he obviously felt pain. But what he didn't know is that she felt it too. "He's your son."

"A useless one," Baron corrected.

Now she only knew anger.

She remembered every time her parents told her how awful she was, how useless, or how embarrassing. And she remembered how she used to look at the floor all the time, thinking that she was not even worth lifting her head high.

She may have hated Adam now, but she couldn't help but be angry at what he's living through, pity him as she pities herself.

She turned to Baron, nothing can stop her now that she saw her prey. "Do you know what you are?" she asked calmly, "you think you're the almighty Baron who has nothing to lose. But I will do it, I will make you feel hopeless and desperate. Killing you will be mercy upon you, I'll make you wish you never stood in our faces, I'll do it," she said, with wild eyes, and a steady voice. And if there was any worry she felt, she was sure she didn't let it show.

When Alana looked at herself in the mirror, she never wished she could be prettier. No. She wished she could be more terrifying. She'd look herself in the eye and would feel the mirror tremble with fear. Her eyes, she liked that they were always sharp like the edge of a knife. it seemed to her like she saw steam flowing inside her iris when she stared long enough, she thought it was fury, rage, or maybe even fear. But here, now, even if her mirror had sworn it itself he was sure she only felt pure, and utter rage.

It was like an oath. A promise she'd fulfill no matter what, and it was like the whole room sensed that too because the room was quiet, not a sound could be heard apart from her heavy breathing.

Baron gulped. "Let Keir talk the girl to let me go." He nervously shifted his eyes to Jenny. "I'll let her go, and we'll talk this out."

She glared at him one last time before she turned to Keir, she tried her best not to stare at his wounded arm and gave him a look, it was an order with their eyes, they always shared this silent language, and somehow they always understood each other.

Keir beckoned to Jenny towards Baron, and Jenny took a step towards them. "Let him go, Ryan."

The man holding Baron let go of him, though he still had his gun aimed at him as he stepped away.

"Now let her go," ordered Alana.

Baron smirked. "No. Alana. I just wanted to show how incredibly naive and stupid you are. I mean I taught you better, how many times did I tell you not to trust anyone? How can you hurt me when I know every move you'd take?"

Keir took a step towards Mirelle, though Baron stopped him shortly. "Take another step and I'll kill her myself."

Keir stopped, in his place but Jenny groaned, "Ryan!"

But before Ryan could move, Baron took the gun attached to his belt and shot him in the chest. Ryan took a few shocked steps back and fell to the floor. Dead.

Mirelle let out a loud cry, and Alana wanted to run to her and get her out of here. She'd done more than that to her, but now she stood helplessly, unable to do anything.

"Get the boy!" Baron yelled to his men gesturing to Dylan.

She nearly vomited on the floor. Everything is going wrong. She knew Dylan could manage that, but the idea of him getting hurt just made her feel more nauseous.

A man caught Dylan and wrapped his arms around him so harshly.

She wanted to kill them all, without mercy. For herself and for her family. And somewhere deep down, she knew she would.

"What now, Keir?" Baron asked.

Keir's eyes never left Mirelle. His face was between pained and scared and something else she assumed was love.

He shut his eyes so tightly, and a tear dropped on his cheek.

Even though she took his strength as a perfect image for herself, she knew he was tired, she always knew that. But now she only knew she wished what she was thinking about wouldn't happen.

Keir dropped to his knees, still clutching his wounded arm, and dropped his head. "Stop this nonsense. Let them all go. I give up." Only his defeated voice echoed through the room.

She looked at Dylan, to see if what heard was right, Dylan's eyes widened. So she knew it was. She didn't know if she should be mad at him for it, or mad at Baron or at herself. But all she knew was that she was mad. Very mad.

"I'll do it. I'll work with you. Just let them leave."

'What has gone to you? ' she wondered. 'You said we had to fight? What are you doing?'

"No!" Mirelle screamed. And Keir shut his eyes even tighter.

Then it happened. And she didn't know if she was falling or if it was just her heart.

Mirelle.

What is he doing? How dare him?

He promised me. He promised he'd stay.

I had to do something and do it now. But I knew I couldn't if that man is holding me that tight. So I breathed and remembered everything Keir said about fighting.

Strike where they least expect.

But I bet he didn't even know I was armed, so I took my knife out, slowly.

I hated this. But I didn't have another choice.

I took the knife, and with all the power I got, I planted it in the man's foot. He let go of me, and I ran to Keir.

Only that it's not that easy. I really thought that was it.

How dumb can I get?

At first, it was like someone brushed past me aggressively. Then there was a burning pain throbbing at my side.

I took a glance at where it hurts, and behold there's a big blood-stain on my white shirt.

Oh, Come on, that was expensive.

I look at the back, to see that man with my kitchen knife in his hand, starting at my side. I put my hand on it, and hold my hand up to my face to see the blood covering my whole hand.

Oh.

Stabbing people is rude.

And it hurts.

I couldn't stand anymore. My legs gave out and I fell, clutching my side, though I knew I was losing a lot of blood already.

I let out a great sigh. Is that really it? Am I going to die? I think I am.

I looked at Jenny, with a smile. Here, Jenny. One cool story to write, I hope you don't forget the part where you mention I had the intelligence of Sherlock Holmes. She should be fine...I'll miss her.

I switched my eyes back to Dylan, I always loved that little idiot. I don't know who will get him Doritos now but...he'll be fine.

Then I looked at Alana, she's a warrior. I knew that from the moment I met her. She survived a lot so... I think she'll survive this too.

I coughed. And lastly, looked at him. They all looked terrified, but him...he was different.

His face was white as snow, He looks like a beast taken away by loss, he was everything between broken and scared. I saw how he was...how a piece of me was broken when I looked at his pained face.

But now...this was each and every type of pain planted in his face. And here I am, for the first time, wanting to do something but can't.

But he's taught how to fight now. Physically and in any way possible. I smile a little at him fighting against the man who held him.

Where do these people come from?

But I couldn't help and let out a cry at that. There was so much I wished we could do together. I wanted to grow up with him, taste new stuff with him, take him to parks and get him vanilla ice cream as we laugh together.

But I guess this is how it ends.

We had enough time with each other, we watched each other enough, we've already gone to parks and we ate a lot of ice cream.

What would I do without him? What if he needs me?

I promised myself that I'd watch over him. And I'll take care of them all. I promise myself that I'd still laugh with them, and be with them. Just...not here.

I looked at Keir, trying to get enough of him as they say, and his hair. oh, his hair.

He'll be fine.

It's getting cold. I wouldn't know if it was because I was dying or because it really was getting cold. I have felt this feeling often. Like my heart itself is shivering, maybe it also feared this moment, maybe it was preparing me for it.

I'm gasping a lot, letting my body try its best at holding on to life. But who am I kidding?

the end lies ahead of me, and there's nothing I can do but wish it won't be cold on the other side as well.

I watch people running and people speaking, and I imagine myself as them, thinking I had too much life already, thinking I still had a lot. But when you're alive you only think of being alive, and here I am, trying to live for some more seconds.

I'm slowly being taken away from life, it's becoming more of an illusion, as if it never happened and as if I never was.

People often die having a smile on their faces. They seem to think they lived enough, they seem to be very satisfied with what they've done, they seem very intrigued to finally let go, to pass, to end.

But...I don't! I want to run away, I want to smile, I want to feel the wind. I don't want to go yet. I don't want these to be my last thoughts, I don't want this to be my last thing to watch. Them grieving me as I'm passing away.

I am the once reckless teenage girl who dreamed of hope and faught everything that stood in her face as the bravest queen would do, but then she realized that death was always stronger than empty high hopes, stronger than pride, and boldness.

My heart physically hurts, I'm heartbroken over how much time was wasted. I still wanted to live. I wanted to feel. I wanted to hold on.

But it seems like life let go of me itself.

Chapter 29

Keir.

Her eyes were a living fire in mine, clinging to them for life. She knelt on her knees but not a flicker of weakness formed on her face, just like she always stood up for me, just like the first day I met her.

I dared to look away from her face to her side, where blood already spread on her body. I snapped my eyes back to hers again with utter terror pulsing through my whole body, I can feel my bones shaking so hard, and my chest burning like it was on fire.

I looked at her, pleading with her not to let go, to do what she asked me to do. But she only smiled, more assuring and peaceful than ever. With tears in her eyes, she fell, her hand holding her wound, blood pouring around her.

She looked every one of us in the eyes. With the smile I lived and fought for, she mouthed a 'goodbye.'

Now, and only now did I realize I was screaming, crying, and fighting against the man's grip, begging him to let me go to her.

"Alana!" I roared.

Alana immediately let go of Adam and ran to Mirelle.

She knelt beside her and lifted her head, she turned to Baron. "You!" she screamed. "What have you done!"

At first, we only smelt it: ash and smoke. I looked around me, the fire was clinging to the curtain of the room, spreading in the whole building. Everyone was screaming and running. Beside it, my mother's eyes looked back at me with horror I'd never seen on her before, she sat there, the wooden sticks she started the fire with were close to her.

"Dylan," I let out defeated. Dylan ran to my mother and grabbed her and ran to leave the building.

The man's grip eased on me a little. And I took that to my advantage and pushed him and ran to her.

Everyone was running out of the building, people were screaming, they were fighting each other to get outside, there was too much chaos, but I only saw her on the floor.

I knelt beside her, not conscious of anything happening around me, I took her head in my hand. And wrapped my arm around her body. Her blood already stained my hands, my clothes, and my face.

"No," I whispered.

She just smiled, held my shivering hand with hers, and took a long breath, "it's okay, I promise."

I shook my head. "Stay with me-"

She weakly cupped my face with her hand. "Do me a favor," she struggled. "One last one."

"...please.."

"Listen to me." She shivered. "Don't stop fighting, Keir. And don't you dare give up for me."

"Stop it. I'm begging you to stop this."

She shut her eyes so tight the tears slipped from her face, "I want to know you're okay when I'm up there." My own tears fell on her face, but she only gave me a weak smile. "I'll be waiting for you. I'll be waiting for you to tell me everything you've done, to tell me How Alana and Dylan fought and how you always were the wisest of them, the adventures you went to, and the new friends you made, the new loves you'd find, what you laughed about when I didn't get to be with you. Everything, I would want to listen to them all."

"Don't leave." I sobbed. I shook her hard so she could wake up.

She shook her head and held my hand to stop it. "Don't give up, and don't blame yourself for this. Remember everything I told you, imagine me there with you because I promise you I will be."

She reached and wiped my tears. "I love you, Keir. I will always love you, not just till death drive us apart." She took a long breath. "It was a wonderful journey, Keir. I...I'd do it all over again. Just...please...r emember me in the life I didn't get to live with you. D-don't forget me."

The fire had already eaten half of the room. So I carried her in my arms and ran.

She's living.

"Wake up, Mirelle!" I yelled in my raspy voice. "Stay with me!"

She was shivering yet sweating, she shook her head weakly. "I can't, Keir."

"Somebody, Help!" I gasped. "Help me!"

She closed her eyes. "You won't- you won't do it outside with me like this. L-Let me go. Leave me here."

I was running so quickly I didn't know it was possible with all the injuries I had. But that didn't bother me. All I thought about was her, all that mattered was her.

What am I supposed to do without her?

"Open your eyes. look at me, I hate this!"

Her lips slightly quirked. "As much as I'd love to, I really can't."

"Just talk to me," I begged. "Please."

"Will you call my parents?"

"Tell them what?" I knew exactly what she meant, it was like a stab to the heart, but I wanted her to talk and not slip away from me.

"That I'm...gone." My eyes blur with tears. "They always loved you. I want you to take care of them when I'm not here. You call them and tell them everything is going to be okay."

"Mirelle," I spoke her name. To let get know that it will live with her. She can't just be nothing in my life, as if she never existed. As if she never touched me. Why did the world have to forget her?

What will I do if I woke up and found emptiness instead? I lived my life inside of her, what and who will I feel when she's gone. I felt her every heartbeat, what will happen if I couldn't anymore? A million times I'll need her, a million times I'd want her between my arms but I won't find her, I'll only cry. If she goes I'll go with her.

It was the warmth I felt when we sat beside each other. Now, how am I supposed to warm myself? Who would hold my hand in the rain? Who would hug me and tell me that it was okay? Who would smile in my face like there's nothing in this world that was worth worrying about? Does she not know that I have no one but her? If she's gone, then I'll just sit in the darkness alone every morning while I think of no one but her, there would be no one else I'd known left for me to think of.

Would I truly hear your voice in the air as they say? Or would I feel your touch as the rain falls? Or is it your embrace warmth that I'd feel in the sun? Would I close my eyes and imagine you were there?

Would I see your eyes in the glass of my windows? Would I wake up every day searching for you? I'd find nothing, wouldn't I?

God, take me if you're going to take her! Don't leave me wandering alone on this earth...please...God.

There was no answer for a long time. and when I looked down at her, her eyes were closed and her breathing was...gone.

And here I am. Once again, left alone with someone taken from me.

Chapter 30

Keir.

I under my breath as I ran through the fire. It was everywhere, but I still ran without it harming me.

My hand tightened on hers as I approached the main door. I kicked it with my legs first, but it still didn't open. I kicked it again, this time harder, and it burst open.

The first thing I saw was Dylan, Alana, and Jenny. They were yelling at someone, something about them wanting to get inside. I looked behind them, and the police were everywhere. "Help! someone help me!"

They all gathered around me, and one of them pointed at my arm. "You need-"

"Just take her!"

They didn't waste time, someone took her from my arms to an ambulance car, and then they made me follow behind.

Mirelle.

When I woke up I found myself in a hospital.

oh no.

I hate hospitals. They smell like...babies and I hate it. There's a lot of blood there, and they have bad food and I also want a pizza. Wait.

I'm alive.

I glance at my side, where a big bandage was placed, and apparently, that was enough to remind me that every single inch of my body hurts.

I turn to look at the side of my bed, and a blood bag was hung from a perch. I cringe and I rest my head back on my pillow. I wonder whose blood that is. Would someone be mad right now if I order pizza? Or maybe ice cream. They give ice cream to sick people.

Keir.

I sat upright, ignoring all the pain that was followed by that. I was relieved when I saw him curled up on the hospital chair, his messy hair falling on his face as he slept peacefully. Then I look at his arm, a big bandage covered his upper arm and others on both his legs.

I remember everything now. And let me tell you it doesn't really feel nice.

Many times, I've seen people die. I've seen people wishing for their graves yet never finding them. I've seen people lose hope in life because they've lost someone, never did I ever think I could be that person. I'm familiar with death, with loss, or that's what I thought.

Seeing your life flashing through your eyes with you thinking you'd leave, at any second. Now, that is what death is: You leave when you wish to stay and live and experience, that's death.

I was afraid, a new kind of afraid. When my eyes only saw him, only saw his full-of-tears eyes. I thought I'd leave him wounded. It didn't hurt me that I'll go as much as it hurt to see them grieve for it. I was afraid of the paths they'll choose for themselves if I go. How odd it is to wish life for someone when you're giving away yours.

Part of me was relieved, that I wasn't alone, that people truly cared for me deep enough that they held to my hand while I fade away, that they ran through a building on fire to save me. That. Is what life is.

Sorrow, grief, happiness, loss, and even death are a part of life. Just walking without knowing where you'll go in life. Loving someone unconditionally, eating ice cream at sunset, reading someone's poems, writing them, eating pizza, exploring through the woods, and nearly getting yourself killed for like the hundredth time, surviving. This is what life is. Live. Live before you go.

I take in his presence. My throat tightened at the sight. How can someone be like this?

His eyes flutter open, and he gives me a tired smile when he sees me, and I find myself smiling too.

He sits. "Are you okay?"

I nodded and gave him a soft smile. "You?"

He nodded. "I'm alright." I thought that was it, so I stayed silent, but he stood up.

I thought he was leaving but I was surprised when he rushed to my bed, kneeled beside it, hurried his face in the sheets.

I pat his head. "I'm okay, I promise," I said with the steadiest voice I could manage but it still came out shaky.

"Please...Please, don't ever do that to me again.."

I managed an awkward laugh. "Well God said not today, you're still getting me a monkey."

For some reason, he didn't find this funny.

Well bad for him I'll make this my whole personality and I'll keep making jokes about it for the rest of my life.

The door opened, and a nurse got inside. That doesn't make Keir let go of me though.

"Good afternoon, Miss Austin!" she greeted. "Thankfully, none of the vital organs were harmed, you just lost a lot of blood, we took care of the wound, and you'll be able to leave in a couple of days."

A couple of days? What am I going to do here?

But I guess it's not going to be this boring when Keir is that clingy to me.

"Thank you," I mumbled with a smile.

She turned to leave but then she halted. "Are you ready for a little visit?" she asks uncertainly.

I nod and I feel Keir groans. She smiles and leaves. The door bursts open again.

I didn't think it was going to be that little visit.

My parents, Dylan, Al, Jenny, and even Lauren came sprinting inside the room.

"You lived, you wierdo!" Al yells.

Both my parents come to hug me so tight, my poor mother cried, and Keir still didn't move. When they looked at him questionably I just shrugged and said, "he's my child."

"Mirelle, I was really scared for-"

"Dylan, honestly, were you scared I'd die or that nobody would buy you Doritos?" I squint my eyes at him.

"Well, I was worried about you, but now when you say it like that..."

"Dylan, everybody saw how you cried like a five-year-old," Al interrupts.

I pout. "You cried?"

He shrugs shyly, "it's not like I'm the only one who lost his mind." He pointed to Keir.

"Shut up," Keir answered so respectfully and I patted his head at that.

They all sat till midnight fell, they didn't shut up for a second.

I was happy to see my parents get along with Lauren. But Lauren wasn't Lauren of course, if you ask me none of them was. And it wasn't better knowing that it was all because of me. I still try to make them laugh as much as I could to lighten the mood.

After a long day, They all finally left, but Keir stayed. Which I was thankful for.

I try to tell myself everything was fine now and that it was fixed, his peaceful face told me that, so I sighed and finally closed my eyes to sleep.

I lived.

I spent two nights at the hospital. if Keir wasn't there I would've probably lost my brain.

it went pretty cool actually. I mean it was either him telling me to stop messing with my IV, or me listing all the reasons why that hospital could be haunted, or how I thought the nurse was trying to kill me, or just me complaining about hating to sit in that stupid bed all day, he did tell he was taking me home after a few hours, but it just too much.

Even after we left the hospital, he kept acting like a mama chicken. and to be honest, I didn't mind, it's not like I didn't want three years of rest.

Lauren left a few hours ago after she had a bit of an....emotional conversation with Keir. I myself cried just hearing them talk. Though I was happy it was finally done, I was even happier to know that Keir's uncle is now in prison.

We decided to take a nap after all of that crying. Did it last though? Of course not.

"I'll get it." He stood up as the knocking grew more impatient.

"No, I'll go. It's okay, you need rest." I ran to the door before he could say anything else.

I opened the door and...Adam.

I was unable to speak, just seeing him made me want to vomit.

"Mirelle," He whispered, "I-"

"You stay away from her and get out of my house!" Keir yelled and I'm sure he woke up the whole house saying this.

"Keir, listen-"

"I don't want to listen to anything you say, get out!"

Adam started to tremble. "Please...Mirelle, tell him."

Does he think he'll get me with tears? Well, yes of course. "Keir... just listen to him. He doesn't want anything else at least just listen."

Keir sighed. "Mirelle-"

"Just five minutes."

Keir didn't speak after that. So Adam did. "I know and I understand what you feel and I know you hate me and I know I deserve it," he sobbed. "But I didn't have any other chance. He made me do it and you know how he forces us to do stuff against our will. It's pressuring, and threatening, he keeps consuming you with every single word he lets out of his mouth. But... He's in prison now. His building is gone and everything he ever had is gone."

That reminds me of Alana. The look she gave Baron that day. It was like a promise she made to remind him of his deeds if he ever forgot them. And it was fulfilled. Yes, Lauren was the one who started the fire, but Alana was the one who got the wooden sticks in the first place.

Adam's voice got raspy as he spoke. "I even- they were going to hurt Mirelle the day she went out to get pizza, but I didn't let them, you remember that right? At first, I only wanted my father to think I'm a good son but when I saw you I didn't think you deserve any of that." He lifted his eyes to all of us now, including Al and Dylan who were awoken by Keir's voice. "Forgive me."

I looked at Keir in a pleading manner. Even if Adam hurt us he's sorry now. In the end...he's just a child who was used by his horrible father. I always think that forgiveness doesn't mean that we forget so I went and stood beside Adam. "I forgive you, Adam."

He nodded and managed a simple smile. Then he looked at Keir.

"Adam," he said. Then he shook his head. "I forgive you, you fool. I really decided I will. Only it's really for your own good that I will ask this of you. If you stayed here with us, I'll hate you, not because I want to, but because I won't help it, these...events will keep replaying in my head more than they already do the moment I lay my eyes on you. I don't forget, as you might have noticed. So please, for your own good, don't let me hate you or hurt you, I forgive you, truly. Let me have this."

Adam seemed as if he couldn't believe himself, he blinked and opened his mouth, "th-thank you, yes! yes, of course, this is more than enough." He smiled softly as he held the door handle behind him, "But...if I may ask this of you, any time, you feel like you hated me less in a way that you can tolerate me, or just anytime you need me, please call."

We smiled and nodded and I said, "sure."

He walked straight out of the woods like the first time he came.

Epilogue

Mirelle.

A leaf falls from the tree I'm resting my back against, and that snaps me back to reality.

I was sitting outside the house, reading what Keir wrote last night because I was too sleepy to read it back then, or maybe he just went on with that because he was too shy to show them to me.

I once was drowning. I was lost inside the darkest waters,unable to breathe or find the surface.As good as a dead man I was,dead also in his heart and feels and sight.

I knew, of course, of the life over my head.How waves crashed boats. How love was lost in flowing glass bottles.How birds painted the skies with their wings.Yet I still could not lift my arms for help.

The waves became my friend; they dragged me inside their coldest hug. I fought it no more, for my arms were not made of stone.

You took a hold of my arms and lifted me up,and I could have mistaken your touch for a mystical creature,if only you didn't seem so scared of touching the monster of the water, scared yet bravest than the strongest wave.

You spoke of hope and light,and I knew Nothing of such, for I saw nothing but darkness and felt nothing but despair,but I found my arms, once again, pushing down the heaviness of the waves as you dragged me up.

'We've reached the surface,' you'd said.And surely, I loved the air, and the sun and the earth,but your eyes were my only rescue,my only hope and light.

I-

I cry when I read them. Even if I read everything he wrote a thousand times they always take my breath away. The way his thoughts curve to metaphoric words on paper for me...he thinks and writes about me, it's his love language, and I never loved it more.

Our love is a connection between two souls, two minds. It was never just making love or flirting for us. It's comforting each other when we cry, it's fighting for each other, it's living for each other, it's seeing everything dark and yet loving it fully.

It's also him laughing at my jokes even though he thinks they're lame. They're not.

"I see someone woke up and chose to steal," a voice suddenly says, and I jump.

I turn to look who it was though I am one hundred percent sure. "What is wrong with you, you scared me!"

Keir comes to sit on the ground beside me and wraps his arms around my shoulders. "Did I now?"

I squeeze both his cheeks and pull away to get up, but of course, he wouldn't let me.

Someone clears their voice. "I...made dinner."

Alana.

Keir sighs and stands up, he stretches his arm for me and I take it. We walk inside with Al. "Next time, don't interrupt us," Keir mumbled to Al.

"Shut up, Keir."

She's a baddie.

After we ate, I took Keir back to sit under the tree, the stars were bright and clear, glowing to make their presence admirable, and the wind felt nice on our skin. I glance up at Keir, he looked like he was one of the stars as he stared at them.

He chuckled softly, and I found myself once again, admiring every part of the sound.

He stops laughing and his eyes run on every part of my face. "I'm so happy I met you."

He's actually going to make me blush. "Careful, Keir. I may be with Baron after all."

"I said I'm sorry!"

Okay, yes he did like thirty-seven times. But is it enough torture though? No. Never. "I mean C'mon, I'd be happy I met me, did you see how I stabbed that guy's foot? I was so cool. I'm definitely telling this to our kids."

He stills but then he sighs. "How many times do I have to tell you not to stab criminals?"

Talk about foreshadowing.

"Okay but I was still so cool, admit it." He didn't answer. so I pinched his arm.

"Ow! yes, Mirelle that was the coolest thing I've ever seen in my whole entire life, but still don't stab anyone ever again."

He's always so aggravated I don't know for what, to be honest.

"If we had children, what would you name them?"

Oh, I know the answer. "D-"

"You're not naming my child Doritos."

"Oh come on!" I act like I'm mad but then brush it off five seconds later because look at him. "Okay, then what about you, Mr. Perfect?"

He smiled as if he's been waiting to be asked. "I want a girl and a boy. Inina for the girl. It means a glimmer of light. And for the boy, Orpheus. It means the darkness of the night. I want them to be a trace of us, like they existed from the little wild Mirelle who always found light in the dark Keir."

Poetic.

Now that was cute. And actually, my heart was playing the ukulele and dancing in Hawaii right now. "Literally no one does that. What kind of names are these?"

"Mind your business I'm going to name my children as I see."

I don't try to tell him that they're mine too, instead, I laugh and I rest my head back on his chest and watch stars twinkling with him.

I savor it. Everything, every heartbeat, every breath. I savor the stars around us, the grass under us, and the little flowers surrounding us. And him.

Everything in my life was put in its place, even if it seemed messy at any time, I like to believe everything was planned from the day I took my first breath, and that everything that is put for us to face, is nothing but blind monsters. Maybe, what we face in life wouldn't make us stronger, but it will remind us of the fighters we are.

It's okay to cry, it's okay to be afraid, it's okay not feel the best, it's okay to not know who you are for now, it's okay to even nearly die. But you can live again, even if you lost a lot of blood. Trust me, I know.

There is always a gift, a congratulation for surviving. Whether it was a person, a smile from a stranger, a good song you love, or even a very very good ranch pizza.

So, free yourself from yourself.

I turn to Keir. "I love you, today, tomorrow, forever. I'm also so happy that I met you, you're the best thing that ever happened to me, Keir. Even if sometimes you seem like you're the stupidest person ever, I love you."

Here it is.

I heard him laugh. "I love you too, Mir," he said and pulled me closer if that was even possible, but then he shut his eyes tightly, the smile vanished from his face, and he dropped his head.

Dylan stood just behind us, playing his violin, with the most emotional look on his face, I couldn't help but laugh. I'll never be done with him, he's everywhere. Minutes later and Al joined, smiling like a baby.

We dance, eat, and laugh till the sun rises.

And the story continues to grow, with love and joy and sorrow and shock and...life.

At the end of the day, I close my eyes and lie down between Keir's arms, and around the people I love. Not in a million years, I would have thought I'd be here. I only saw them and hoped we'd stay like this, I saw Keir and hoped he'd fight well enough, and now I know that Keir saw me and hoped he'd fight well enough as well.

Spoiler alert: he did just that.

So maybe, just maybe, hope is truly the thing with feathers after all.

Milton Keynes UK
Ingram Content Group UK Ltd.
UKHW020920291124
451807UK00013B/1036

9 781918 122473